THE JESUS FILE

Desmond Leslie

Desmond Leslie has exposed the Easter story to an entirely original interpretation by imaginatively recreating the sensational documentation that would have surrounded the trial of Christ if modern bureaucracy had been avai...le.

The File reveals the whole story from Christ's arrest to his execution through intelligence reports, the trial transcripts, private letters, confidential memoranda, army orders and records of police interrogations. Basing his account closely on the synoptic gospels, Desmond Leslie reveals all the characters, particularly Caiaphas, Pontius Pilate, and the centurion in charge of the crucifixion, in a fresh and dramatic light.

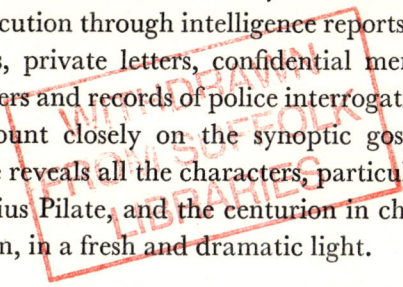

Desmond Leslie was born in 1921. He is the son of Sir Shane Leslie, the Irish poet and biographer, and brother of Anita Leslie the authoress. His previous book, *Flying Saucers Have Landed,* became a world bestseller and was translated into seventeen foreign languages.

ISBN 0 283 98137 7

Cover design by Peter P......

SIDGWICK & JACKSON
£3.75
U.K. ONLY

By the same author
FLYING SAUCERS HAVE LANDED

THE JESUS FILE

by

Desmond Leslie

✝

SIDGWICK & JACKSON
LONDON

Published in Great Britain 1975
by Sidgwick & Jackson Limited
Copyright © 1975 by Desmond Leslie

ISBN 0 283 98137 7

Printed in Great Britain by
A. Wheaton & Company, Exeter
for Sidgwick and Jackson Limited
1 Tavistock Chambers, Bloomsbury Way
London, W.C.1A 2SG

CONTENTS

Foreword and Acknowledgements   8

The Jesus File is discovered   11

THE JESUS FILE

Letters and intelligence reports concerning Jesus, son of
Joseph   17

Court transcript from the trial of Jesus   31

An account of the startling results following the sentence to
crucifixion of Jesus of Nazareth   91

startling results follow

No further action?   203

FOREWORD AND ACKNOWLEDGEMENTS

In compiling this dossier, I have been greatly assisted not only by the four original biographers of Jesus the Joiner's Son whose concept of Love as the prime dynamic of the universe transformed at least the western half of this planet, but also by a number of scholars whose painstaking research into conditions prevalent in the Middle East during the first century A.D. have enabled me to reconstruct a detailed and authentic historical background to the trial of Jesus and its aftermath, which I have deliberately reset in more modern idiom. For the story is timeless, repeated age after age: goodness sacrificed to political expediency.

In particular, I must credit Stewart Perowne, whose invaluable works: *The Life and Times of Herod the Great* and *The Later Herods, The Political Background of the New Testament* (Hodder & Stoughton, 1957 and 1958) fill in so many gaps left by the all too brief accounts of Matthew, Mark, Luke, and John.

I am also deeply indebted to Professor Ethelbert Stauffer whose careful tabulation of ancient Jewish law in his works: *Jerusalem und Rom im Zeitalter Jesu Christi* (Franks Verlag, Berne, 1957) comprises 123 clauses of "The Blasphemy Act" under which laws Jesus was legally indicted and convicted. Legality and morality then, as now, are not necessarily related.

I must also acknowledge the life-work of the late Mgr Ronald Knox, S.J., whose English New Testament translation I have called upon for the actual words of Jesus. Whilst colloquializing others such as the man born blind from birth and the Roman centurion whose servant was healed, I leave the words of Jesus in their original – they could never be changed.

Stewart Perowne and others agree that certainly during the active ministry of Jesus, politically dangerous in the eyes of the Establishment, both Jewish and Roman Intelligence would have infiltrated secret agents into the Nazarene Party keeping both Temple and Praetorium actively informed. But "Agent XXIV, Marcus Sylvanus, of Roman Military Intelligence" is of course not an historical character, although his counterpart or counterparts most surely must have existed, and the effect upon them of the momentous happenings in the six weeks from Easter to Pentecost must, to say the least, have been traumatic. How many defected from the line of duty as a result of what they heard or actually witnessed we shall never know. Yet, it could be assumed that some are numbered among the first martyrs. Today or yesterday, no government takes kindly to agents who come up with the wrong answers.

Apart from using occasional modern idiom, my only other license, for which this whole book depends, is to imagine an abundance of cheap paper at the disposal of the Establishment, when in fact the Roman Civil Service managed to function with extraordinary efficiency, merely using waxen tablets. These could be erased after use rather as we now erase the magnetic tapes of our dictaphones. Only items of major importance merited the costly business of permanent record on papyrus, parchment or stone; which could well have made life simpler for all concerned!

Regarding dates. It is now generally assumed that Jesus was born in 5 B.C.; otherwise he could not have been born during the reign of Herod the Great, who died in 4 B.C. and whose paranoid fear of the prophesied king who would usurp him prompted the massacre of the Holy Innocents and the flight into Egypt of the Holy Family. However, to avoid confusion, I have remained with the traditional date of A.D. 1, corresponding to the Jewish "Year of the World 3760" and its Roman equivalent then expressed as: "Ab Urbis Conditae 753", from the founding of the City of Rome; an event which could be accurately pinpointed in time, whereas the creation of the world could not.

But Roman dating, just to make things more difficult, has the disquieting habit of running backwards. Each month is divided into three parts: the Nones, Ides, and Kalends, with a confusing countdown of days prior to each of these. So that for example, "the *fifth* day before the Nones of June" ("ante diem quintum Nonas Junias", or "a.d. V Non. Iun.", for short) is followed by "the *fourth* day before the Nones of June", (a.d. IV Non. Iun.) which is why some of the following documents will appear to be dated in the wrong order. Such a cumbrous system helps explain why Romans never achieved much in mathematics.

Assuming Jesus died on Good Friday, in A.D. 33, then the one date of which we can be absolutely certain is that it was on the 14th day of Nisan in the Jewish year 3794, as Nisan 14 is the Eve of Pesach or Passover which date, like Christmas, never varies. Thus, its Roman equivalent (subject to calendar reforms, errors and corrections) could have been somewhere around 2 April, or a.d. IV Kal. Apr. A.U.C. DCCLXXXVI.

This brings up the contentious question as to how so much could have taken place in so short a time – less than twenty-four hours between the arrest in Gethsemane on Thursday night and the execution on Friday afternoon. Into this brief period are compressed a plenary hearing before the Court of the Sanhedrin; a brutal police interrogation with mental and physical torture (personal humiliation and disorientation techniques so beloved by today's police forces); a dawn hearing in the Roman Court to the incommoding of the Governor-General; a remand to the Herodian Court at the Hasmonaean Palace where Herod Antipas was in residence for the Passover; at least two private "examinations in chambers" by Pontius Pilate, thoroughly dissatisfied by the whole proceedings; a severe judicial scourging as a hoped-for compromise sentence; a great deal of legal argument, pressure and counterpressure between Jewish and Roman authorities, capped by a well-primed riot; yet still leaving time for Jesus to undergo the long agony of crucifixion preceded by the slow death-procession to Calvary. All this is traditionally said to have occurred between late-night on Maundy Thursday and five, or, at latest, five-thirty p.m. Good Friday. For the body had to be removed from the Cross and all burial rites complete before six p.m. when the Passover commenced and all such activities had by law to cease.

Knowing the time that courts, any courts, take to decide *any-thing* (especially in a court where, according to the evangelists, witnesses were in violent disagreement and many had been suborned) has given reasonable grounds to suspect that the whole process from arrest to death occupied a considerably longer period. Some authorities such as Wesley Tudor Pole put it as much as three weeks. However, as this book is based on the account given in the Synoptic Gospels, whose story value cannot be bettered, I am using traditional dates, even though it sets a formidable task for my busy "scribes" whose "Classified" and "Secret" documentation may now be opened for the first time!

1973   D.L.

HOME OFFICE VIA IMPERIA
ROMA Insula IV

To Publius Flavius,
H.M. Keeper of Archives,
OFFICE FOR COLONIAL AFFAIRS
FORUM XX, ROMA, Insula I.

Pridie Nōn. Sept.
A.U.C. MLXXXII*

My Dear Publius,

The enclosed File which I am forwarding to your Department (unread) to wit, File No. I/CXII/BI/VI/A was in all probability consigned to our own Records Section in error, shortly after the execution by Titus of "The Final Solution to the Jewish Problem".

When the Jerusalem Imperium was dismantled and transferred to Rome, and that tiresome little thorn removed from Roman flesh, there was inevitably a modicum of confusion. Thus, with the great amount of loot, baggage, documents and other impedimenta, many files ended up in the wrong departments and, even at this late day and age, continue to be turned up from time to time.

It is therefore more than likely that you too may have in your good keeping files more properly the purview of the Home Office' in which case be so good as to remit them to us as soon as possible. For, with the proposed move of the Administration to "New Rome'; on the Bosphorus (Yes, it *is* going to be named "The City of Constantine" – whatever else did you honestly expect?) it is essential that we have all our records in perfect order prior to the olympian task of crating and packing.

As you well know, we in the Home Office pride ourselves on the accuracy with which we keep all our affairs – even such ancient and academic documents as these herewith enclosed.

I very much hope we shall be seeing you at Julia's next weekend. It has the ring of a good party. We might even take a trip down to Ostia and try out Decimus's new boat?

Sincerely
PAULUS AGRICOLA
H.M. Controller of Records

ENCL: I File

---

* Note: September 6 Anno Domini 329 or 1082 Ab Urbis Conditae "from the founding of Rome".

OFFICE FOR COLONIAL AFFAIRS
FORUM XX ROMA Insula I

To Paulus Agricola
H.M. Controller of Records
Records Dept.
Home Office
Via Imperia, Insula IV

ante diem VII Id. Sept.
A.U.C. MLXXXII

My Dear Paulus,

Many thanks for that load of dusty documents!

Just what we need when we have not sufficient transport even for essential and important records! I was on the point of seeking the Minister's permission to throw the whole lot into the furnace when I observed (as you apparently did not) that certain portions of the files on 'Jesus, one-time prophet and former joiner's assistant', are classified: CONFIDENTIAL, SECRET, TOP SECRET, and even EYES ONLY.

Of course, under the Official Secrets Act the statutory period of one hundred years has long expired so that I may be tempted (given the time and energy) in the next few days to dip into it and see what murky secrets had to be withheld lest they should have endangered the Realm at the time of Tiberius Caesar (of glorious and immortal memory).

Yes, I intend to get to Julia's if time and Flavia will allow.

Should the files contain anything interesting, scandalous or amusing I may bring them along as well.

Until then,

Yours
PUBLIUS FLAVIUS
H.M. Keeper of Archives

OFFICE FOR COLONIAL AFFAIRS
FORUM XX ROMA Insula I

To Paulus Agricola,
H.M. Controller of Records,
Records Dept.
Home Office,   *a.d. XIX Kal. Sept.*
Via Imperia, Insula IV   *A.U.C. MLXXXII*
Re File No. I/CXII/BI/VI/A

Dear Paulus,

Sorry I could not make it to Julia's – too much packing to be supervised – but glad to hear the boat was a success.

Now look! There's something a little peculiar about File No. I/CXII/BI/VI/A which I gather you did not take time off to peruse being so commendably concerned with the orderliness of your office. However I have given it rather more than a cursory reading and am somewhat perturbed by its content.

Doubtless you will recall the strange rumours in circulation some four years ago concerning the Milevian Bridge where it was said H.I.M. Constantine saw a vision in the sky, cruciform in shape, and having something to do with the conquest of the world?

I do not wish to put too much in writing; rather would I see you at earliest opportunity, for I have it on Highest Authority that Rome, now so liberal in its toleration of pluralistic religions, could rapidly be approaching an era when "Mores" may give place to "Fides" – if you follow my meaning. I am not the only one who would be sad to see the demise of our merry old Gods, their enjoyable and complex lovelives, their frolicsome bacchanaliae, and best of all that excellent arrangement with mortals whereby Faith is entirely optional!

But since this "vision" our Glorious King is a little too keen on anything and everything appertaining to the Jewish prophet who met with such an ignominious end, so that I would urge you to drop

13

everything and to give the said File your immediate and urgent appraisal. To which purpose I am returning it herewith UNDER SEAL and by Emperor's Messenger to be given into your hands personally.

You will readily guess what I have in mind. The cardinal question is this – will it do us, our jobs, not to mention our heads, any good if we were to submit this disturbing collection of documents to Caesar?

I shall make no further move without consulting you.

Yours,

PUBLIUS FLAVIUS
H.M. Keeper of Archives

ENCLOSURE UNDER SEAL

HOME OFFICE VIA IMPERIA
ROMA Insula IV

a.d. XIX Kal. Sept.
A.U.C. MLXXXII

PERSONAL BY COURIER

Dear Publius,

A quick line to acknowledge safe receipt by Emperor's Messenger of "the file in question".

At your request I am cancelling all appointments for the rest of the day. I shall read it and give you my immediate reactions.

I quite agree with you. Say and do nothing! Speak to no one until we have ascertained its import and value – if any.

Sincerely,

PAULUS

PS. I have glanced through it. Don't move! Don't speak to a soul, I must see you URGENTLY.

P.

S. P. Q. R.

THE
PRIVATE AND PERSONAL
FILES OF
HIS EXCELLENCY
PONTIVS PILATVS
GOVERNOR GENERAL
OF
IVDÆA

THE ECCLESIASTICAL COURT OF THE GRAND SANHEDRIN

WARRANT FOR ARREST

To MALCHUS, the Officer-in-Charge and his Several Officers of The TEMPLE POLICE (Temple Precinct) Jerusalem

Know ye, All men by these Presents that WE, JOSEPH CAIAPHAS, High Priest of Jerusalem and Primate of All Israel Send GREET-ING, and command that you omit, not by any reason of any liberty in your Precinct, but that you enter the same and lay hands on

Jesus Son of Joseph (onetime Joiner's Assistant)
Of *The Town and Urban District of Nazareth*
in the *Tetrarchy of H.M. Herod Antipas*

And that you have his body before the several ELDERS AND RULERS of this HOLY COURT to answer unto US concerning divers offences trespasses and contempts of which he has lately been indicted and to answer unto US upon certain articles presented against the said, and have you there then this WRIT and render unto US an account of your doings.

Given Under Our Hand
This day and year hereinunder set out
JOSEPH CAIAPHAS BEN SETH

> By the court, etc.
> Nisan 2 in the
> Year of the World 3761

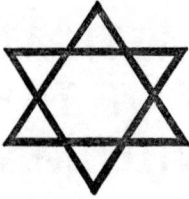

THE ECCLESIASTICAL COURT OF THE GRAND SANHEDRIN

MOST URGENT

JUDGE'S MEMORANDUM

To: DATE: *Nisan* 13,3794
His Excellency, PONTIUS PILATUS, By Imperial Warrant, Governor General of the Province of Judaea, Lord President of The Supreme Court, etc. etc.

Your Excellency,

Owing to the imminence of the Feast of the Passover and subsequent closure of the Courts, I am enclosing for your most urgent and immediate attention the Court Transcript and papers relevant to the Hearings, now concluded, concerning the Traitor, and self-confessed Blasphemer and Apostate, one Jesus, son of Joseph. We most urgently request *immediate* ratification of the Death Sentence by virtue of the Powers vested in your noble self by the Supreme Authority of Rome.

We have, as you will doubtless be aware, by the very size and length of said transcript, given to the Condemned an extremely fair and lengthy hearing; under, I might add, conditions of considerable difficulty and provocation. The Accused not only declined all legal assistance (same having been offered and procured by none other than the Honourable Joseph of Arimathea) but obdurately refused to defend or speak for himself until the conclusion of the Hearing when We Ourself questioned him, only to elicit from his very lips the most dreadful blasphemy, arrogating unto himself the forbidden and secret NAME of the Most High God of Israel. He therefore stands self convicted and self condemned under "The Blasphemy Act", as per Sections: 16 and 18.

Therefore has this Holy Court ruled (subject to your Upholdment and Ratification) that he shall be punished in full accordance with Sections 21, 22, 23, (incl:) of the said Act

18

viz: 21   "The Convicted Blasphemer shall die"

22   "His body shall be hung from a cross"

23   "Before 6 p.m. on the day of execution the body of the Blasphemer shall be taken down from the cross and buried without honour."

Thus, to save Your Excellency the tedium of protracted study of the Transcript, and because of eminent advisability of having sentence carried out before the Feast of the Passover, I am further requesting that the Imperial Supreme Court agree to the immediate issue of a "Writ of Horaath Schaar" [*Instant Justice*] to that he may be put to death in time for the Passover for reasons upon which I shall briefly enlarge:

(1) Section 71 of the Act states: "In exceptional cases the High Priest of the Grand Sanhedrin shall be empowered to over-ride obstructive rules so as to put a swift and radical end to Apostasy by means of a "Writ of Horaath Schaar".

(2) We deem this to be an exceptional case qualifying under Section 71.

(3) We further enclose for your most excellent consideration an additional Schedule of Civil Offences over which the Ecclesiastical Courts have no jurisdiction but which more properly come within your purview. These offences constitute direct threats to Caesar's Peace, His Crown and Dignity and must be taken into consideration when sentencing:

I summarize:

(1)   Treasonable utterances against Caesar.

(2)   Conspiring and threatening to depose the Lawful Head of State (i.e. Caesar and/or Herod) and to usurp their Position, their Power, their Crown and Dignity.

(3)   Conspiring and inciting divers persons to withhold the taxes properly and lawfully payable unto Caesar.

(4)   Causing H.M. Collector of Taxes (Jericho Collection) to desert his office and to join the ranks of his followers, thereby leaving office of the said Collection untended, and causing serious detriment to the Inland Revenue.

(5)   Practising Medicine without due Qualification or Licence.

(6)   Catering without a Licence.

(7) Riotous Assembly.
(8) Incitement to Riot and Civil Disobedience.
(9) Divers and sundry offences liable to cause a breach of Caesar's Peace.

As you will doubtless see from (1), (2), (3), (7), (8) above, the prisoner is *extremely dangerous*. He has recently had himself proclaimed "The Messiah", not only in the Capital but in many suburbs and outlying country districts. His following grows daily with alarming rapidity. He has barn-stormed the whole Province in an open and unabashed bid for power. So confident is he of fomenting successful rebellion that he was, until today, working up the rabble-rousers in the Capital itself. From my own sources of intelligence (which have been closely co-operating with Roman Intelligence) we were led to suspect that this Feast of the Passover, now upon us, was to be the signal for a national uprising. Therefore we arrested him and brought successful Proceedings *in the nick of time*.

It is our further respectful opinion that a firm hand shown NOW, and the removal of this demagogue before the Feast reaches its height will ensure total collapse of the movement and a speedy return to law and order. There is nothing more discouraging to would-be "reformers" as the spectacle of a Public Crucifixion (particularly when the City is packed with visitors and pilgrims) as Rome well knows!

I therefore look forward most confidently to Your Excellency's fullest support, certain as I am that this will undoubtedly earn the highest commendation from the Colonial Secretary and, ultimately, from Caesar Himself.

HAIL CAESAR!
I remain Your Excellency's Most Loyal and Obt Svt

JOSEPH CAIAPHAS, D.D.
High Priest of Jerusalem
Primate of All-Israel
Lord Chief Justice of the Courts
Ecclesiastical
Lord President of the Council of
The Grand Sanhedrin, etc. etc.

ENCLS: 3
1 Copy Official Court Transcript.
1 Copy Intelligence Report No. V/I.C. (*SECRET*)
1 Copy Background Report No. II I.C. (*CONFIDENTIAL*)

MILITARY INTELLIGENCE

Report Forma
Classification: SECRET
Copies Only To   (I)   H.E. The Governor General
              (II)   Director, Military Intelligence
            (III)   Central Intelligence, Rome
           (IV)   His Grace, The Primate
From   Marcus Sylvanus, Cpt. (Agent LXVI)
Subject   Jesus, son of Joseph (alleged prophet and former joiner's assistant)
Code Name of Subject: "SALVATOR"

Report No. V/I.C.

Date anti diem VIII Id. Feb. DCCLXXXVI

SALVATOR has been kept under strict surveillance for the past two years by Agent LXVI and two other officers of The Special Services, posing from time to time as willing listeners to his speeches, and, as in the case of this Agent, infiltrating the inner party caucus.

While SALVATOR is not of himself considered politically dangerous, it is the opinion of the Department that there is considerable danger of his power and following being used by professional agitators, rabble rousers, anarchists, and hooligans acting from purely selfish and destructive motivation.

Having regard to the psycho-emotional factor of the hope-stimulation-impact of his doctrines upon the native credulity and, *in particular*, the national prophet-inspired messianic wish-dream and the (computed) 60/40 probability of nation-wide disorders arising therefrom, SALVATOR should be seriously considered as a Security Risk of considerable magnitude.

Owing to the recent recurrence of religiously inspired rioting and looting, the sectarian differences and hatreds, the General Officer Commanding the Xth Legion has reinforced the Jerusalem Garrison, bringing it up to full Riot-Contingency Strength, which will doubtless prove more than adequate to preserve law and order. This must be borne in mind, throughout this report even though SALVATOR's basic doctrines are non-violent and pacifist by nature.

21

The Department's Finding can presently be summarized as follows:

(I) SALVATOR is an accomplished conjuror.

(II) He has definite apparent healing powers; though in most cases these could be attributable to auto-suggestion, hypnosis, and the psychosomatic nature of most of the ailments allegedly treated, i.e. "Casting out of evil spirits", blindness, lameness and palsy dating back to birth or to traumatic experience, which type of ailment comprises the majority of his alleged cures. Whether these are of temporary or lasting duration cannot at present be established owing to shortage of personnel assigned to make a study in depth of same after the event.

(III) Another factor to be considered in evaluating his hypnotherapeutic abilities is "the will to be healed"; for there is an established relationship between the intensity of the desire to be healed and the efficacy of the cure. For instance, on numerous occasions observed and recorded, the sufferers have been heard to say: "If only I could touch but the hem of his garment, healing grace will flow out to me." In such cases it is considered that the attitude of the sufferer would constitute a major factor in the ensuing "miracle". Indeed, SALVATOR himself has frequently confirmed this: e.g. "Your FAITH has made you whole" or "Your FAITH has healed you." In this respect it is important to note that universally accepted tenet of the Jewish Religion that all illness (mental and physical) originates from sin and wrong-doing. Recognizing this, SALVATOR normally prefaces his ministrations by assuring his "patients" that their sins have been forgiven. This would be of prime importance, particularly in the cleansing of lepers (considered to be the rejects and outcasts of their God) but in such cases the immediate replacement of leprous tissue by firm and healthy flesh is not readily explainable in terms of present medical knowledge. Nor, as far as can be ascertained, are there any precedents for this kind of phenomena. But the conclusions (above) pointing to psychosomatic causes need not be invalidated, but should rather strengthen the premise that his ability to stimulate the subconscious is exceptional, and of sufficient power to effect or to simulate a complete cure.

(IV) The multiplicity of food (loaves and fishes) on two occasions has not yet been satisfactorily answered; though it is more than possible that a number of persons had concealed upon their persons divers articles of nourishment which, in the superheated atmosphere of "brotherly love" and "fair shares for all" which he so successfully promoted, would have caused them to feel compelled to share their concealed rations with their companions, thus giving rise to the impression that more food was magically produced at his command. (cf. the native legends of miraculous feeding by means of "manna from heaven" dating back to their nomadic days: a race-memory which could have had a certain bearing on the situations in question.)

(V) The psychological impact factor of all these cures or alleged cures throughout the Province should be borne in mind and carefully assessed, were he to turn political and place himself at the head of the imminent rebellion which the natives have read into their prophetic writings, and which many of them hope will now take place under the direction of SALVATOR.

But it must be firmly stressed that, when asked to take up this leadership, he has given reprimanding answers, and has stated quite categorically that his "kingdom (i.e. the Province) is not of this world"; doubtless to safeguard himself against possible reprisals by the authorities should he be charged with incitement.

(VI) Less easily explained however, are two cases of corpse reanimation – one from a funeral bier, and one from a tomb in which the corpse had been interred for a period of four days. The two subjects in question were presumably not dead but in states of deep catatonic trance, evincing all the symptoms of death, i.e. cessation of respiration, heart action, and all normal bodily functions. But the method of their revival was so simple as to defy any normal medical explanation. SALVATOR in Case A merely took the subject by the hand and ordered a reawakening, and in Case B had caused the tomb to be opened (illegal) and without actually entering same, called out to the dead man to awake and emerge. The details of this case have been supported by many witnesses and must be taken as substantially true and correct, but at the time of writing there is insufficient scientific information at hand for a complete analysis.

(VII) The most puzzling factor, tending to indicate a negative rebellion-minded orientation, is his completely apolitical sense of opportunity. Time and again he has settled in a town, where, by means of amazing cures and stimulating addresses he has incited the crowds to a state of frenzied adulation. At which point, had he so ordered, they would have followed him and died for him to a man. But on each and every occasion just as he had obtained the requisite marginal support to initiate an insurrection, he quietly disappeared from public view. Witness, for example, his recent visit to Jericho where he stirred the whole town to a frenzy of religious fervour, and then, as if deliberately to throw away his political advantage, took lodgings in the mansion of Zaccheus, the most detested man in the whole town. Zaccheus is H.M. Collector of Taxes (Jericho Collection), renowned for his extortion, corruption, and falsification of Revenue returns. This completely annulled his short-lived local popularity. But the effect on Zaccheus was said to be traumatic. He is now reported to be founding a charitable trust to which he is bequeathing his entire ill-gotten fortune! He has also resigned his office, leaving the Jericho Collection in a state of considerable confusion.

(VIII) From these many lost opportunities it would appear that either: (a) SALVATOR is completely lacking in elementary crowd-influence-acumen, or (b) that he genuinely entertains no political or personal ambitions. In the latter supposition it might be surmised that his deliberate disappearances are calculated to produce a deeper impact, so that his words will be remembered longer than he who spoke them. He has, in fact, stated that though the universe should pass away, his words would not.

(IX) We are inclined to believe that he does not particularly relish personal adulation and that he feels that the teaching he has to impart is of greater importance than the mere person of the teacher; and that he is well aware that given half a chance, the mob would promptly deify him, which would be bad for his purpose, and irritating to the Emperor who, quite rightly considers that one god-in-human-form is more than sufficient for this planet at any one time. ENDS REPORT.

Classification: SECRET   **Prepared by:** *MARCVS SYLVANVS*
For Official Use Only   AGENT LXVI

MILITARY INTELLIGENCE

Report Forma
Classification: CONFIDENTIAL
Copies to: General availability all Officers M.I.
From: Caius Crassus Cent. (Agent XXI)
Subject: "SALVATOR"
Report No. II/I.C.
Date: ante diem V Id. Mai. DCCLXXXV

Personal Background and Previous History

SALVATOR, according to Registrar of Births, Deaths and Marriages (Bethlehem Urban District), was born in the Fifth Year of the reign of AUGUSTUS CAESAR during the General Census proclaimed by His Late Imperial Majesty, which occasioned his mother, Miriam (Maria) to travel with her then husband, Joseph Ben David to the said town of Bethlehem where said Census registration was being conducted. Some difficulty in obtaining accommodation resulted; all hotels and guest houses being completely full. However, it is reported that the Manager of "The Bethlehem Inn" contrived to find them quarters in the stabling section of his premises where the child was delivered by normal birth.

It may be noted that this was the time of the Comet which had aroused considerable scientific (and other!) interest, and was at the time of speaking, completing 18°51' of arc per 24 hours. Reports and rumours that the Comet appeared to be arrested in transit and remained motionless directly over the said "Bethlehem Inn" are groundless and misleading. (We append hereto the Official Report from the Royal Observatories, Caesarea, which gives completely satisfactory and correct explanation for these erroneous rumours.)

[*See Notes I and II attached.*]

NOTE I: There were at the same time other reports of unusual celestial and astronomical manifestations; all of which, on proper investigation, proved entirely groundless and without scientific foundation. But it should be recalled that the planet Jupiter (the "Royal Star") was then in conjunction with Saturn-Sabboth (the Star of David or Israel) giving rise to excitable speculations by astrologers and augurers that a royal, or even Messianic Personage was being born to Israel. (See Appendices XI/XXII "Messianic Predictions and Prophecies" and Vol. II "Digest of Semitic Prophets (abridged)" for verification.)

NOTE II: Likewise, reports by simple shepherds and peasants concerning unidentified objects, lights in the sky, and even of "angelic" or "celestial" choirs are readily explainable as simple meteoric showers. Meteorites frequently produce curious "out of this world" humming, buzzing or swishing sounds which, to the untutored ear and superstitious oriental mind could so readily be interpreted as angelic voices singing: *"Glory to God on high,* etc". This was to be expected, taking into account the general tensions and expectations caused by unscientific astrological predictions about that time. **End Notes.**

Maria, his mother, was highly pregnant at the time of the wedding, an occasion of considerable concern as Joseph's family claim blood descent from the royal house of David and are most highly respectable and orthodox.

Both families are well connected and have between them a number of influential friends and relatives, not the least of which is the Hon. Joseph of Arimathea, and it is generally held that the match was arranged (though somewhat tardily) with the obliging and elderly spouse in an attempt to protect the family's good name. Indeed, Joseph, proprietor of "Joseph and Son, Joiners", operated a successful and skilled cabinet-making business in Nazareth, their home town (a town which has completely scorned any of the pretentions of their dubious son: SALVATOR).

However, inquiries made in Nazareth reveal that SALVATOR was a rather unusual boy, highly intelligent and very well liked by his playmates and companions who gave him the nickname of "Joy". But his tremendous gaiety would be offset by long periods of introspection and silence. He would wander off into the hills for days on end. Sometimes he would sit and meditate. Other times he would be found laughing and talking to the animals, the birds and the trees. He had a profound love of Nature and beauty, and it is more than likely that these early experiences, coupled with his knowledge of the scriptures, was the initial cause of putting grander ideas into his youthful head.

He was in these times a considerable worry and puzzlement to his family who admitted they failed to understand his motivations. Things came to a head when, in his twelfth year, they made a pilgrimage to the capital where he promptly got lost for a period of three days. His mother reported him as missing, and pursued a frantic search, only to find him sitting in the Temple lecturing the learned doctors and theologians: engaging them in flights of mysticism, remarkable for one so inexperienced.

He was in the midst of a profound discourse as to the inner meaning of the scriptures when his mother arrived, scooped him up, and scolded him soundly for the worry and anxiety he had caused. Quite undaunted, this precocious child was reported to have answered: "Don't you know I must be about my Father's business?"

to the amusement and delight of those sages whom he'd been engaging in discourse.

There are some doctors extant who can still recall that occasion: one, an Initiate of the Hermetic Mysteries, was at a loss to understand how a mere boy of twelve summers could be in possession of so much knowledge of the Ancient Wisdom, unless he had access to the secret archives of the Alexandrian Library where the mysteries of the Universe are revealed only to the chosen few.

Yet, records show that the boy had only once left the Province, for a brief visit to Egypt, when he was a mere babe; unable to read or write.

Another, a visitor from the Far East, had proclaimed him to be a Bhodhisattva (or Great Teacher) sent to redeem the world of its ignorance and folly. He expressed the view that he was a reincarnation of the divine Krishna, a view that shocked the Orthodox who asked him to leave the premises forthwith.

As to what happened to him after that, there is little concrete evidence, only hearsay.

Some say that he remained in Nazareth where he qualified as a Master Carpenter and Cabinet-maker. But there were long periods during which he was absent from his home town.

We have not had the opportunity of questioning the Hon. Joseph of Arimathea to date, but it has been reported that he took his kinsman SALVATOR on a mineral-carrying ship of the merchant navy to visit West Brittania where the Hon. Joseph had valuable interests in tin mines. During this visit the boy is reported to have visited Glastonburium, an ancient and holy place, sacred to the religion of the First Men, and also the great Solar Temple and Observatory standing in the middle of the huge plain of Sarum and to which holy men are said to come from all parts of the world on certain solemn occasions.

But again, these reports cannot be verified at the time of writing and must be regarded as apocryphal.

From majority to his present age, little is known of him. But it is generally believed he entered to the Order of the Essenes and studied in their monasteries – possibly at Qumran – under the renowned, but totally secluded master who is only known to the outside world as "The Teacher of Righteousness". This would be consistent with his later public pronouncements and behaviour. For it appears that he has revealed a number of doctrines (which might be called: *"Theologically Classified"*) previously restricted only to initiates of this order, a fact that could account for the hostility he has aroused in higher religious circles.

About three years ago he was formally initiated in a "water ceremony" performed by his cousin John the Baptiser *q.v.* These ceremonies took place in the River Jordan and consisted of ceremonial immersion and ritual cleansing, symbolic of spiritual regeneration; after which he set out upon his nation-wide tour of preaching and faith-healing, which has continued without respite up to and during the time of present writing.

NOTE: Said John was later executed by the Tetrarch (with some trepidation it seems) under pressure from his then wife about whom he had made some discourteous and offensive remarks. **End Background Report.**

Classification: CONFIDENTIAL
For Official Use Only
Prepared by: *C. R. CRASSVS* AGENT XXI

See appended report, supplied by Royal Observatory—

Q.

ROYAL OBSERVATORY
CÆSAREA

Ante diem tertium Kal. Feb. Anno Urbis Conditae DCCLIII

The recently reported STELLA NOVA has not at the time of writing been positively identified, but is considered to be a Major Comet of elongated elliptical orbit, with Perihelion Distance considerably less than One Astronomical Unit – that is to say, within the orbit of the Earth.

Owing to its proximity, its mean daily motion has been considerable. Now, in recession, its coma is somewhat less bright than a star of first magnitude. No tail has been reported.

About four weeks ago, during its period of maximum brilliance, certain confusions arose giving rise to a number of erroneous statements and concepts. At this period, owing to a series of optical illusions (which to date have not satisfactorily been explained), the daily rate of motion appeared to be reduced from 18° 51' as from Pridie Nonas Decembras to a mere 3° 30' on a.d. VIII Kal. Dec., thence to zero degrees as from a.d. III Kal. Dec. until Nonis Jan. giving it the appearance of a stationary body with an apparent ninety degree vertical ascension directly over the Town and Urban District of Bethlehem. During which period, the Instrumental Observational Facilities of this Establishment were most thoroughly checked and recalibrated, with exhaustive tests made for possible malfunction, precession, and other errors. *All such tests proved NEGATIVE.*

However, there is at present no evidence to hand which in the aggregate would tend to suggest the likelihood of any extraneous factors such as the intrusion of a secondary body or bodies of sufficient mass to produce velocity fluctuation and/or orbital eccentricity that would account adequately for the phenomenon as reported; thus leaving us to conclude that (pending evidence of instrumental malfunction) there took place a culminative observational error to which ice-crystal layer-refraction allied with high altitude temperature inversion would be contributory causes.

PATRICVS PLVRIMVS
For ASTRONOMER ROYAL

XII/DII/B

30

ECCLESIASTICAL COURTS
CITY OF JERUSALEM

COURT TRANSCRIPT

(OFFICIAL COPY)

In the matter of: Jesus, Ben Joseph, (self-styled Prophet and one
time Joiner's Assistant)
Date: Nisan 13. 3794
Case No. 238/B/10/4
Archive No. 7462/EC

**Copy to H.E. The Governor General
for his immediate attention!**

TO THE GREATER GLORY OF GOD, THE PROMUL-
GATION AND PRESERVATION OF THE TRUE LAW OF
THE HOLY PROPHETS AND THE MAINTENANCE OF
CAESAR'S PEACE, HIS CROWN AND DIGNITY.

Whereas   I, Zerubbabel Ben Nathan, *Clerk* of the holy court
of The Council of the Grand Sanhedrin do hereby
solemnly swear:—

That all These Matters hereinunder set out, inscribed and recorded
do constitute a true and accurate account to the jot and tittle of all
the Proceedings of the said court relating and appertaining to the
Trial Indictment and Hearings, and the Verdict and Sentence so
passed upon

JESUS BEN JOSEPH

Court Seal
In Witness thereof   *ZERUBBABEL BEN NATHAN*, CLERK

DATE   Nisan 13, in The Year of the World 3794

COURT TRANSCRIPT
(OFFICIAL COPY)

Case No. 238/B/10/4.   Date Nisan 13 3794

CLERK: Hear ye, hear ye, all ye who have aught to do with my Lords, The Rulers and Elders of the Ecclesiastical Courts of the Grand Sanhedrin, draw nigh and give your attention! Be upstanding in Court for My Lord, the Most Reverend Joseph Caiaphas, Doctor of Divinity, High Priest of Jerusalem, Primate of All Israel, Lord Chief Justice of the Courts Ecclesiastical, and Lord President of The Council of the Grand Sanhedrin.

JUDGE: Most Reverend my Lords of the Sanhedrin, pray be seated. Have we our full Plenum as required by Law of two and seventy Rulers of the Council of the Grand Sanhedrin?

CLERK: One absent, M'Lud. The Honourable Joseph Arimathea prays to be excused by reason of his kinship with the prisoner.

JUDGE: Oh yes – most proper, most proper indeed! Has a deputy been sworn in?

CLERK: A Deputy Elder has been so impressed and sworn, M'Lud.

JUDGE: Reverend my Lords, I have called this Special sitting of the nigh court as a matter of extreme urgency. Tomorrow is the Eve of the Passover and it is in the interests of the Government and the True Religion to have the whole matter concluded as swiftly as possible! Call the arresting officer.

CLERK: Call the arresting officer! (*He is called.*) What is your name?

WITNESS: Malchus. Servant to His Grace the High Priest.

JUDGE: Did you, Malchus, arrest the prisoner?

MALCHUS: I did, My Lord.

JUDGE: Can you see the prisoner in this court?

MALCHUS: That is he, My Lord, Jesus Ben Joseph, whom I arrested as per my orders, and brought here before you.

JUDGE: I understand it was dark at the time of the arrest? Can you be sure it is he and none other?

MALCHUS: Indeed I can be sure. This same is Jesus Ben Joseph. I carried out my orders and accompanied the picket detailed to arrest him. As it was dark we required some extra identification from one who knew him very well.

JUDGE: And who was that?

MALCHUS: One of his own followers, the Party Secretary and Treasurer in fact – one Judas Iscariot.

JUDGE: How was the prisoner to be singled out from the group? What arrangements had you made with this Judas Iscariot?

MALCHUS: Judas said to us: "He is none other than the man whom I shall kiss. Hold him fast."

JUDGE: Did he?

MALCHUS: Did he what, My Lord?

JUDGE: Did he kiss him, you idiot?

MALCHUS: Yes, My Lord, he did. He went up to him and said: "Hail Master!" Just like that. And the prisoner said: "Judas, would you betray the Son of Man with a kiss?" And then his followers endeavoured to resist arrest and to obstruct the officers in the course of their duty. And one of them drew his sword – that man there – that man slinking out of the court, that man at the back cut off my ear! *Quick! Stop him!*

JUDGE: We are not concerned with your ear at this stage. Let that man leave the court.

CLERK: It appears he has already done so, M'Lud!

JUDGE: Obviously a case of guilty conscience. But doubtless he will come before another court to answer for his conduct.

MALCHUS: But my Lord! He cut off my ear!

JUDGE: Your ear appears to be in perfectly sound condition. It also appears to be where it should be – attached to the side of your head. I trust there hasn't been another miracle? (*Laughter*).

MALCHUS: Er – yes, My Lord. Prisoner said: "Put up your sword, for those that carry the sword shall perish by the sword!"

JUDGE: Did he, indeed? I am tired of these irrelevant and frivolous remarks. The Court is satisfied the prisoner has been properly identified. Has the prisoner been arraigned?

CLERK: No, M'Lud.

JUDGE: Then arraign him!

THE ARRAIGNMENT

CLERK: Prisoner, hear the charges! That you, Jesus Ben Joseph, of the Town and Urban District of Nazareth in the Tetrarchy of H.M. Herod Antipas on diverse occasions between the years of the World 3790 and 3794 wilfully, maliciously, and knowingly did contrave the law against heresy, apostasy and blasphemy, contrary to the form of the Statute therein made and provided and more particularly sections 1, 6, 7, 8, 16, 18, 53, 59 of the "Act for the Suppression and Punishment of Blasphemy, Heresy, Apostasy, False Prophecy, Wonder-Working by the Power of Belial, Incitement to Rebellion, and Defiance of the Authority of the Rulings of the Grand Sanhedrin".

(1) In that you did, wilfully and knowingly break the law of the Sabbath contrary to Section 1 of the said Act and therein recited as:

Section 1: "that whosoever, knowingly and willingly breaks the law of the Sabbath Day and/or any other commandment of the Torah has despised the Word of the Lord," wherefore under –
Section 2: "on first conviction he shall be cautioned" and under
Section 3: "on second conviction he shall be punished by death."

(2) That you did on multiple and divers occasions practise medicine without a licence by means of quackery and witchcraft and did cause to be healed or appear to be persons suffering from divers diseases, contrary to Sections 53, 54, 55, of the said Act and therein recited as:

Section 53: "The False-prophet may be sent by God to tempt Israel."

and per

Section 54: "The False-prophet is the instrument of hell imbued with the spirit of Belial whose powers enable him to perform miracles; such power to perform miracles being no *a priori* proof of Divine Inspiration."

Wherefore under

Section 55: "The False-prophet shall be convicted by the Grand Sanhedrin and executed in Jerusalem."

(3) That you did on divers occasions also practise medicine on the Sabbath Day contrary to Sections 1, 2, 3 of the said Act heretofore recited.

(4) That you did wilfully, knowingly and shamefully mock and repudiate the legal authorities and/or their decisions, contrary to Sections 6, 7, 8 of the said Act and herein recited as:

6. "The Grand Sanhedrin in the Temple of Jerusalem hands down decisions in the Name of God. God himself respects the said decisions."

and wherefore under Section:

    8. "Disobedience of the rulings of the Grand Sanhedrin shall be punishable by death."

(5) That you did on divers and multiple occasions conspire to pervert believers from the True Faith and from the Laws of the Prophets, contrary to Sections 39, 59, 60, 61, 62, and 65, 66, 77, 78, 81, and therein recited as:

    39. "The preacher of apostasy is a Son of Belial who tries to convert God's people to apostasy by persistent agitation."

and per Section:

    59. "If a man be suspected of apostasy there shall be an inquiry made regarding the circumstances of his birth, for the bastard inclines towards rebellion and blasphemy."

and per Section:

    60. "For so long as a bastard shall lead a devout life there shall be no adverse comment on his birth."

and per Section:

    61. "Once a bastard has become an apostate the circumstances of his birth shall be frankly and mercilessly exposed."

and per Section:

    65. "The Grand Sanhedrin in Jerusalem is the sole legal Authority with power to pass death sentences in all cases of apostasy, subject to ratification by the Supreme Court of Rome."

and per Section:

    66. "All trials for apostasy must be conducted before Plenary Session of the said Grand Sanhedrin."

and wherefore under Section:

    77. "The apostate shall be executed for the Greater Glory of God."

and per Section:

    78. "The corrupter of the people shall die lest the corruption spread further."

and per Section:

    81. "If, before their execution, the convicted shall admit their guilt and repent, they are certain of God's forgiveness and a share in the Bosom of Abraham."

(6) That you did on or about the third day of the month of Tebeth enter the Temple with a band of followers and did cause malicious

damage to sacred property, wantonly and sacrilegiously, and did cause wilful damage to the property of certain persons therein lawfully employed and did obstruct and disrupt the lawful trans- actions of authorized bankers, money-changers and purveyors of sheep, oxen, doves and sundry sacrificial flora and fauna contrary to Sections 7 and 13 of the said Act and therein recited as:

7. "Whosoever shall defy the Authority of the Grand San- hedrin shall be punished by death."

and per Section:

13. "Whosoever defies the officiation priests in the Temple shall die."

(7) That you did on or about the twenty-first day of the month of Adar, in the Outer Court of the Temple threaten to destroy the entire fabric and structure of the said Temple and, thereinafter, within a stated period of three days, to rebuild reconstruct and otherwise restore the said structure and fabric, contrary to Sections 1, 6, 7, 8, 13, of the said Act and herebefore recited.

(8) That you did on divers occasions hold up to mockery, ridicule, odium and contempt the priests and elders of the said Temple engaging them in specious rebellious and contemptuous arguments, contrary to Sections 7 and 13 of the said Act, heretofore recited.

(9) And lastly that you did publicly and openly arrogate to yourself Divine Honours in that you did claim to be the Messiah, the Christ, the Son of God, and that you did openly and blasphemously arrogate unto yourself "The Most Holy Name of God" contrary to Sections 16, 18, 21, 22, and 23 of the said Act and therein recited as:

16. "Whosoever shall take the Name of the Lord in vain is a blasphemer,"

and per Section:

18. "Whosoever arrogates to himself divine honours or rights is a blasphemer"

and wherefore under Section:

21. "The convicted blasphemer shall die."

and per Section:

22. "His body shall be hung from a cross."

and per Section:

23. "Before six p.m. of the day of execution the body of the blasphemer shall be taken down from the cross and buried without honour."

JUDGE: Prisoner, you have heard the charges. How do you plead?

CLERK: Prisoner, you will answer M'Lud!

JUDGE: Prisoner appears to have lost his tongue. Yet I understand he was eminently voluble on sundry other occasions. (*Laughter.*)

JUDGE: The Clerk will enter the plea of the prisoner as "Not Guilty".

CLERK: Very good, M'Lud.

JUDGE: Clerk, enquire if the prisoner is represented.

CLERK: Let him who is representing the prisoner come forward, draw nigh, and declare himself on record . . .

CLERK: No man doth offer himself, M'Lud.

JUDGE: I understand that learned counsel had been engaged by the Honourable Joseph Arimathea to plead on behalf of the prisoner.

CLERK: Prisoner has declined assistance, M'Lud.

JUDGE: Prisoner, you have not availed yourself of the assistance of learned counsel which we understand has lately been offered you, we would urge and caution you that you consider carefully your replies to the questions shortly to be put to you. And that you weigh carefully the import of your answers in the light of the charges laid before this holy court.

PROSECUTOR: May it please Your Lordships of the Sanhedrin, the Prosecution will prove beyond all possibility of doubt that during the last three years the prisoner has traversed the width and breadth of the Province on a rampage of insubordination and conduct prejudicial to good order and the Laws of the Prophets. His claims are arrogant and blasphemous in the extreme. We shall shortly call witnesses who will testify that he has not only defied the Authority of the Sanhedrin, obstructed the course of justice, ridiculed the Priesthood, bringing them into odium and contempt, but has, furthermore, destroyed sacred property and even threatened to bring down the entire mighty fabric of the Temple itself.

He has, by means of witchcraft and satanic powers healed, or appeared to heal, numerous of the Emperor's loyal subjects suffering from divers and sundry diseases, thereby corrupting their true Faith and holy allegiance to the one true Church of Israel.

By such means he has desecrated tombs, calling back the apparent dead to a semblance of life. He has practised medicine without a licence and his purported successes have sorely aggrieved the skilful, dedicated and qualified Doctors of Medicine, and the Fellows of the Imperial College of Surgeons whose true and qualified skills have thereby suffered ridicule and contempt. Furthermore, to compound his felony, he has frequently practised his quackery and satanically inspired so-called medical skills on the Sabbath Day, and when properly rebuked has made insolent and arrogant answers implying that all in Holy Orders are so mercenary, so corrupt, that they would perform any forbidden task on the Sabbath Day for personal profit and gain or for the avoidance of monetary losses.

The prosecution will also show that he has catered without a licence, not to one, but to many thousands of persons requiring nourishment but too idle to have made previous and adequate provision as laid down in the Law. Once again he has compounded his felony by catering on the Sabbath Day making insolent and irrelevant answers when rebuked by duly lawful Authority. He has obstructed the course of justice even to the extent of preventing the Rulers of the Temple from carrying out execution by stoning, of a woman taken in adultery; properly convicted and sentenced under the Law. His entire conduct during the past three years has been one of open rebellion and contempt not only for the Church but for Caesar. He has urged the non-payment of taxes lawfully levied, and has on at least two occasions disrupted the lawful operation of H.M. Office of Inland Revenue, inciting, subverting and causing H.M. Collectors of Taxes to vacate their posts to follow his corrupt and heinous practices, thus leading to the closure of their regional offices to the very serious detriment of H.M. Revenue. And he has, on several occasions incited the withholding of taxes, lawfully payable to Caesar.

He has toured the Province preaching blasphemous and heretical doctrines. When questioned as to his authority for such infamous and impudent behaviour he has claimed a divine dispensation, claiming a direct mandate from the Most High God, thereby setting at naught the Governance and Mediatorship of the Holy Priesthood.

The court will hear first-hand witnesses who will tell, word for word, the text and substance of his wicked addresses. This court will hear how he has engaged ordained members of the priesthood in insolent rhetoric, making them appear foolish and ignorant in the sight of the uneducated masses, thereby defying and setting at naught their lawful and God-given authority, and how he has frequently and publicly insulted them in their Holy Orders, making them a laughing stock.

I need hardly tell this holy court of the grave and serious nature of these offences, nor need I remind them that for the majority of such offences, the penalty as laid down by Law is death. (*Interruption.*) And as if these were not sufficient, he has, during the course of his grand tour of corruption, encouraged and urged on by those he corrupted, and by ignorant and wilful misinterpretation of holy scripture he has allowed, nay, encouraged the notion to take root, yea and to flower, that there exists a relationship between the person of the prisoner here, the wretched, obdurate and humbled . . .

JUDGE: Counsel will refrain from personal remarks. It is for the court to decide on a prisoner's state of obduracy or humility.

PROSECUTOR: My Lord! You have broken my train of thought!

JUDGE: You were saying, Learned Counsel?

PROSECUTOR: Your interruption has broken my thread. I must beg your Lordship not to interrupt . . .

JUDGE: You were saying, Learned Counsel?

PROSECUTOR: I was trying to say that an idea has grown up that he is the Messiah.

JUDGE: Well, why didn't you say so in the first place?

PROSECUTOR: I was *trying* to point out that this idea grew up gradually, and, though initially denied by prisoner, continued to gain ground, until last Sunday, when the prisoner implied open admission of messiahship by taking and driving away (without the owner's consent, needless to say) a *white she-ass* upon which he rode triumphantly into the Capital. I need hardly remind the learned and reverend Members of the Sanhedrin of the implications and significance of the white she-ass. Nor need I recall to learned doctors of holy writ that one of the prophetic signs by which the coming Messiah shall be recognized is that he shall enter the holy city riding on a white she-ass.

JUDGE: Are you referring to last Sunday's demonstration?

PROSECUTOR: I am, M'Lord. Without the owner's consent he took and rode away a she-ass down the main road into the city at a particularly busy time of day causing obstruction and delay to traffic. Not only his followers but many hundreds of hooligans, nationalists and demonstrators also took part, thereby defying the ban on political processions, and causing damage to the ornamental palm trees lining the route; wantonly and maliciously tearing down the branches, waving them in the air, casting them before him and shouting slogans.

JUDGE: What slogans?

PROSECUTOR: Hosanna! Blessed is he who comes in the Name of the Lord! Blessed is the King of Israel!

JUDGE: Referring to King Herod?

PROSECUTOR: Hardly, M'Lord. It is our submission they were alluding to the prisoner. By this open gesture, as well as by recent public pronouncements, the prisoner has openly and brazenly declared that he is none other than the Messiah, the Son of God, the, Holy Redeemer of Israel. (*Interruption.*) But! – but! – but! – worse, I regret is to come! Much worse. (*Interruption.*)

CLERK: Silence in court!

PROSECUTOR: Witnesses will be brought before you who will testify on their most solemn oath that he has arrogated to himself the Powers and the Holy Name of God. Not, mark you the Holy Name, lawful in everyday usage. Not, mark you, even the Holy Name as allowed only when addressing the Most High in personal prayer. But he has used, and claimed for himself – Oh I dare not go on . . .

JUDGE: Proceed, Learned Counsel. Do not distress yourself.

PROSECUTOR: My Lord . . . he has used the NAME . . . I dare not and may not pronounce it, for it is pronounceable only by the High Priest himself, and then but once a year in the sacred privacy of the "Holy of Holies" – the most secret and sacred NAME which My Lord alone is entitled to pronounce prostrate on his face within the said Holy of Holies. (*Interruption.*)

JUDGE: You are excused. The court knows well enough to what NAME you refer.

PROSECUTOR: Thank you, My Lord. I tremble that I might have inadvertently been led to speak blasphemy.

JUDGE: You have spoken well, Learned Counsel, and as your Father in God I assure you that you have committed no sin.

PROSECUTOR: My Holy Father in God is most reassuring. I stand gratefully before him.

JUDGE: Do you have witnesses to this terrible matter?

PROSECUTOR: I do, My Lord, and they most urgently seek your guidance as to how they shall relate prisoner's very words without themselves falling into grievous sin.

JUDGE: I see. We had better deal with the problem as and when it arises. Would you perhaps, care to deal with the charges in order, reserving the final and most serious count till last?

PROSECUTOR: That is exactly how the prosecution had hoped to be allowed to treat them, but owing to the sudden urgency of this case, My Lord, witnesses are still being gathered together. With the court's permission I would deal with each count as and when necessary witnesses become available.

JUDGE: Then pray do so.

PROSECUTOR: Call the Reverend Uriah Ben Eliphas.

CLERK: Call the Reverend Uriah Ben Eliphas. (*He is sworn.*)

PROSECUTOR: What is your name, Rabbi?

WITNESS: Uriah Ben Eliphas.

PROSECUTOR: And your profession?

WITNESS: Doctor of Divinity.

PROSECUTOR: A Doctor of Divinity. Learned in the scriptures, conversant in the prophesies of holy writ?

WITNESS: I hope so. I've studied them most of my life.

PROSECUTOR: So you would feel competent and unashamed to testify before this holy court, composed of your spiritual superiors?

WITNESS: In all humility, yes.

PROSECUTOR: Excellent, Reverend Eliphas! Now, can you please tell this holy court where you were on the 21st of Adar?

WITNESS: I was in the Outer Court of the Temple.

PROSECUTOR: A most fitting place for you to be, would you not agree?

WITNESS: I would indeed.

PROSECUTOR: Very good. And can you tell this holy court what you saw and observed in that revered place?

WITNESS: Yes. I came up behind a group of men whom I later learned were Party Members, and one of them said. "Oh Master, just look at these great stones! What a splendid fabric!" He was referring, of course to the magnificent masonry recently completed by Our Most Noble King Herod.

PROSECUTOR: Of course.

WITNESS: Then their leader replied: "Do you see all this vast fabric? There will not be a stone of it left on another. It will be all thrown down."

PROSECUTOR: Do you see in this court, the man who made that alarming statement?

WITNESS: The prisoner in the dock.

PROSECUTOR: Jesus, son of Joseph?

WITNESS: The very same.

PROSECUTOR: Now think carefully! I ask you once more – did he say "*It* will all be thrown down?"

WITNESS: He said "it".

PROSECUTOR: He did say not say "*I*" will throw it all down?

WITNESS: No.

PROSECUTOR: He did not say that he, the prisoner, would *personally* throw it all down?

WITNESS: Why, no. I'm sure he said that *it* would be thrown down.

PROSECUTOR: You're sure of that?

WITNESS: Quite sure.

PROSECUTOR: Very well, you may stand down. Call the next witness, er – Scribe Benjamin Ben Amos.

CLERK: Call Scribe Benjamin Ben Amos. (*He is sworn.*)

PROSECUTOR: You are Scribe Amos, and your occupation is, I take it, a Temple Scribe?

WITNESS: Correct, sir.

PROSECUTOR: Now, Scribe Amos . . .

WITNESS: He's got it all wrong. I heard it quite differently.

PROSECUTOR: In what way differently?

WITNESS: Well he said "I shall destroy this temple, and in three days I shall build it up again."

PROSECUTOR: Did he indeed?

WITNESS: Oh, definitely.

JUDGE: Are you quite sure of that?

WITNESS: Quite sure, Your Grace.

JUDGE: On oath you are prepared to differ from the testimony of the Reverend Rabbi?

WITNESS: It's my job to hear all right, My Lord. Otherwise I'd not be a Scribe. Accuracy and efficiency, that's our watchword.

PROSECUTOR: Would you concede perhaps that the reverend witness had misheard the actual words?

WITNESS: I only know what I heard, sir.

JUDGE: He definitely said that he, Jesus, would personally destroy our magnificent Temple?

WITNESS: He did, My Lord.

JUDGE: And did he indicate the means whereby he'd accomplish this monumental task of destruction?

WITNESS: He said something about its enemies laying it about and not leaving one stone upon the other.

JUDGE: Doubtless, he would require some assistance.

WITNESS: But he did say he would rebuild it in three days.

JUDGE: Amazing! Considering it has taken 3,000 craftsmen forty-eight years to date, and is not yet finished. But, I suppose we must at least concede him his intention to make good the damage? (*Laughter.*)

PROSECUTOR: My Lord, this is all entirely irrelevant! We have all heard this witness declare that the prisoner *personally* threatened the total destruction of religious property – nay, of the holiest shrine in all the world. My submission rests on those exact words *"I will destroy this temple!"* and with all due respect to the former reverend witness, the court must accept the testimony of one whose profession, the taking of dictation and the making of accurate transcription, demands the highest degree of accuracy and clarity of memory.

JUDGE: Doubtless, Learned Counsel, doubtless! But are you quite satisfied that the testimony of these two witnesses concurs?

PROSECUTOR: In essence, My Lord.

JUDGE: Is that enough?

PROSECUTOR: I would think so. Unless we are splitting hairs.

JUDGE: This court does not split hairs. You are aware, are you not, that Section 69 of the Act stated unequivocally: "The evidence of at least two witnesses is required for corroboration in all cases of apostasy"?

PROSECUTOR: With very great respect, that is exactly what we have obtained.

JUDGE: And you are aware, are you not, that Section 70 of the same Act plainly lays down: "The incriminating evidence of the said witnesses must coincide in minute and incidental details." Now, are you satisfied that the testimony to date does in fact coincide in minute and incidental details?

PROSECUTOR: In my humble submission I would say, yes.

JUDGE: Oh, come come, Learned Counsel, there is a flagrant contradiction in the content and import.

44

PROSECUTOR: With the very greatest respect, My Lord, I would like to point out . . .

JUDGE: Have you any other witnesses to this event?

PROSECUTOR: Plenty, My Lord.

JUDGE: Then if you wish to establish your case to the requirements of the Act hadn't you better call them?

PROSECUTOR: I was about to do so, My Lord, but first I would like . . .

JUDGE: Your junior appears to be trying to attract your attention.

PROSECUTOR: Oh, thank you, yes. (*Whispers with junior.*)

PROSECUTOR: My junior informs me, My Lord, that there is some measure of disagreement among my intended witnesses and that under your Lordship's ruling it would be wasting the court's time to proceed further on this count. Therefore I should now like the court to consider even more serious offences committed at about the same time, wherein he created an obscene disturbance within the holy precincts, destroyed sacred property, committed assault and battery, causing grievous bodily harm to persons going about their lawful business – the servants of most reputable firms dealing in the supply and sales of religious furnishings, pious tracts, holy offerings, and assorted sacrificial flora and fauna, firms who have, for generations, performed their public services in the Outer Court, to the honour and glory of God, and to the benefit of international pilgrims. All of them I might add are licensed annually by the Sanhedrin and all of them *fully paid up* in their Temple Dues and Licences! Call the Manager of the First City Bank of Jerusalem.

CLERK: Call the Manager of the First City Bank of Jerusalem. (*He is sworn.*)

PROSECUTOR: You are the Manager of the First City Bank?

WITNESS: That's correct. Temple Branch.

PROSECUTOR: Temple Branch. Of course.

WITNESS: Never had any trouble before.

PROSECUTOR: Never any complaints?

WITNESS: Well – there has been some criticism of our exchange rates, and the commission deductable in changing foreign currency. But that is normal banking practice.

PROSECUTOR: Certainly it is.

WITNESS: Bankers have got to live.

45

PROSECUTOR: Indeed they have.

WITNESS: Just like everyone else. Got to make a living.

PROSECUTOR: Just answer the questions please. Pray tell us, Manager, tell us in your own words what happened on that morning of the third day of Tebeth.

WITNESS: I've never seen anything like it. The prisoner here bursts into my offices followed by his long-haired mob of hooligans. Without the slightest provocation from those of us who were legally and correctly going about our normal business he starts abusing and beating us.

PROSECUTOR: How did he beat you?

WITNESS: With a whip of knotted cords.

PROSECUTOR: How very distressing for you. Did you suffer greatly?

WITNESS: Indeed we did, sir. I was black and blue. I had to be helped into this court room. I'm still weak from shock.

PROSECUTOR: What else did he do?

WITNESS: He overturned our counters, threw the ledgers around, terrorized my staff.

PROSECUTOR: Had you given him any provocation? Called in his overdraft perhaps?

WITNESS: Good gracious me no! This man never had a penny to his name.

PROSECUTOR: He had never availed himself of your excellent banking facilities?

WITNESS: Never. I wouldn't have him as a customer, even had he come to us. It is the policy of the First City Bank of Jerusalem . . .

PROSECUTOR: Quite! Now tell me, did he or his followers take anything?

WITNESS: I don't think so. They threw the cash boxes around and scattered a number of coins, but I wouldn't go as far as to say they helped themselves to anything.

PROSECUTOR: Was any of the cash, so thrown around, later found to be missing?

WITNESS: We retrieved the greater part of it. But you know what it is when money rolls about and the crowds join in?

PROSECUTOR: I don't, but I follow your meaning. The prisoner did not in fact steal anything, but owing to his disgraceful conduct enabled other persons to purloin some of your ready cash?

46

WITNESS: That is well put. His protest seemed to be directed against the mere presence of a bank within the holy precincts. He shouted at us: "My house is a house of prayer. You have made it a den of thieves!"

JUDGE: I wish to make a note of that. . . he did say "*My* house"?

WITNESS: "*My* house", My Lord. His exact words!

PROSECUTOR: Yet the banking facilities exist within the Temple for religious and pious purposes, do they not? So that gentile coinage, bearing graven images forbidden under the Commandment shall not be used to buy sacrifices, but shall first be converted into the special currency of the Temple free of all impious and pagan inscription: so that the sacrifices can then be bought without transgressing the law?

WITNESS: Exactly.

JUDGE: Do you think he was protesting against your commission rates?

WITNESS: I really couldn't venture an opinion, My Lord.

JUDGE: What are your commission rates?

WITNESS: As I said, the normal. It's standard practice.

JUDGE: What are they?

WITNESS: You want me to give quotations?

JUDGE: What are your commission rates?

WITNESS: They're perfectly all right. They're 25% normally. And $33\frac{1}{3}$% for holidays and special feast days. Bankers have got to make a living.

PROSECUTOR: Of course they have!

WITNESS: Yes of course we have. My directors were very disappointed to note the adverse publicity and criticism. My directors always wish to know their client's requirements.

PROSECUTOR: Of course they do.

WITNESS: It was most unjust calling us a den of thieves.

JUDGE: Did he not also say: "*My* house is a house of prayer?"

WITNESS: "My house", My Lord. His exact words.

JUDGE: As if he owned the place?

WITNESS: Precisely.

JUDGE: As though you were trespassing on *his* property?

WITNESS: My Lord has expressed it most succinctly.

JUDGE: *My* house! I wish to make a note of that . . . Learned Counsel, has there been a medical report?

PROSECUTOR: Yes, My Lord. Three most able psychiatrists who witnessed some of his behaviour, not only on this, but on other occasions, have given as their unanimous professional opinion that he is possessed of a devil.

JUDGE: That would not necessarily diminish his responsibility. It has been laid down that a man does not become possessed of Beelzebub unless he allows Beelzebub to enter in; that is unless he is sufficiently weakened by sin to allow the penetration of his soul by evil entities. For the consequences of which he remains liable. I should like the reports for later study.

PROSECUTOR: They are in your file, My Lord.

JUDGE: Oh yes, so they are. Thank you.

PROSECUTOR: Thank you, Manager, you may leave the stand. Call the First Cashier of Armenian Express. (*He is sworn.*)

PROSECUTOR: I shall be brief. Do you recognize the prisoner?

WITNESS: I do.

PROSECUTOR: Has he ever assaulted you?

WITNESS: Oh grievously! My leg hurts and I can hardly concentrate on my duties any more. Oh it was dreadful, dreadful!

PROSECUTOR: Did he assault you on the third day of Tebeth within the Temple precincts?

WITNESS: Oh yes, terribly, terribly. And he tore up the travellers' cheques and the counterfoils and scattered them in all directions. We still haven't sorted out the mess. My poor clerks and cashiers have been working overtime trying to get duplicates and put the ledgers straight.

PROSECUTOR: Did this rampage of destruction end with your premises?

WITNESS: I don't know. No, I don't think so. No, he ran like an avenging fury. The Bureau of Exchange next door suffered similar desecration and spoliation.

PROSECUTOR: Dreadful!

WITNESS: Oh yes dreadful, too dreadful! I haven't been able to sleep since!

PROSECUTOR: You have the court's deepest sympathy. Are we distressing you too much by making you recall these terrible events? Would you like to rest now?

WITNESS: Thank you, sir, you are so very kind and considerate.

PROSECUTOR: Usher, assist this poor, poor gentleman. Support him to the exit.

PROSECUTOR: One more witness, My Lord. The Chief Auctioneer of the Temple Livestock Marts.

CLERK: Call the Chief Auctioneer to the Temple Livestock Marts. (*He is sworn.*)

PROSECUTOR: Can you tell the court what happened on the third day of Tebeth.

WITNESS: There was bloody murder. He opened the pens and stampeded our cattle.

JUDGE: Who opened the pens? Who stampeded?

WITNESS: Him in the dock there. The prisoner.

JUDGE: Thank you. Carry on.

WITNESS: It was one of the best days too. Cattle prices fetching record prices, owing to the seasonal demands, and the shortage during the last bad breeding season. Why even weanlings were making the price of last year's prime. Sheep too, hoggets and wethers knocking up prices like spring lamb. Then suddenly there's the father and mother of all uproar. About fifty head of Shorthorn Pollies go charging across the auction ring, knocking down the drovers.

JUDGE: What on earth are "Pollies"?

PROSECUTOR: I believe they constitute a generic term for any form of multiple cross-bred cattle, My Lord.

JUDGE: I see. Proceed.

WITNESS: Well, about fifty or more pollies go charging across the ring knocking down the drovers. It was lucky people weren't trampled to death. Then came the sheep, hundreds of them, bleating and rushing about. Poor little things. Some of them ran full tilt into the Court of Sacrifices and smelt the blood. Well you know what it's like when they get wind of their own blood? Panic! Sheer panic. Parts of the court are always a foot deep in blood, especially when there's a big feast coming up. That's why we have the stepping stones to reach the altar. The sheep drenched in blood! The flies and bluebottles rising in swarms! The sheep screaming with terror! Why, I've never seen a more outrageous and horrible desecration to a holy place! Made me positively sick. We dropped a packet I can tell you! Some of the beasts weren't fit to be sacrificed and had to be destroyed.

49

JUDGE: You have applied for and received compensation?

WITNESS: Oh yes, thank you very kindly, My Lord, Your Grace. We have indeed. You have been more than generous. I would like to take this opportunity on behalf of myself and the Guild of Temple Auctioneers to place on record our appreciation and gratitude of the lavish compensation we received – so promptly too. Handed to me as I entered this court. Every penny we lost, plus a bonus. We are more than grateful.

JUDGE: While the Temple is gratified that you consider yourself satisfactorily recompensed, it is irrelevant to the case and will be struck from the record.

WITNESS: But My Lord, we would like . . .

JUDGE: Unless Learned Counsel has any more questions to address to you, you may stand down.

PROSECUTOR: No more questions, My Lord.

JUDGE: Does the prisoner wish to question any of these witnesses before they are dismissed?

CLERK: Speak up, man!

JUDGE: By the silence I take it that you have no questions.

PROSECUTOR: I would like to call the Keeper of the Aviaries, if My Lord pleases.

JUDGE: As you will.

CLERK: Call the Keeper of the Temple Aviaries. (*He is sworn.*)

PROSECUTOR: What is your occupation?

WITNESS: I'm in charge of the sales of sacrificial doves and pigeons.

PROSECUTOR: Did you too suffer damage on the third day of Tebeth?

WITNESS: I'll say we did. Half our stock got loose and was never recovered.

PROSECUTOR: Where is your missing stock?

WITNESS: Have you been in our part of the Temple recently?

PROSECUTOR: I can't say that I have.

WITNESS: Then you'd know right enough if you had. Up in the high pillars, that's where they are, and if you come there I suggest you wear something on your head or you'll know all about it. (*Laughter.*)

PROSECUTOR: This is no laughing matter. I am quite sure that My Lord and the Reverend Elders of the Grand Council are fully satisfied as to the commission and gravity of the outrages so vividly described by witnesses. Their testimony is fully confirmed by the reports of the Temple Police. Of course it is possible to take the view that the great and sacred Temple originally built by King Solomon, now restored and enlarged by King Herod, is just another building, and that damage and assaults upon some of our most cherished religious and business institutions, with behaviour striking at the very roots of our civilization, amount to a mere misdemeanour?

It could possibly be argued that any agitator, rabble-rouser or self-appointed messiah has the right to insult the sacred memory of our fathers – Abraham, Isaac and Jacob and the laws of Moses our Deliverer, and is at liberty to challenge the authority, even of Caesar himself – under whose gracious protection our laws are upheld, our trades flourish and our women and children walk abroad, un-molested? Such may be the case. But I submit that what most concerns this holy court is not so much the material damage – grave though it be – but the purport and intention as determined by the prisoner's exact words: "My house" – the prisoner's house, i.e. the Holy Temple. But to whom does the Holy Temple belong? To the prisoner? Nay, to the Most High God of Israel and of All the World.

JUDGE: Learned Counsel!

PROSECUTOR: M'Lord?

JUDGE: Are you, by any chance summing up?

PROSECUTOR: Not that I'm aware, M'Lord.

JUDGE: Then I'd like you to become so aware, and to confine your activities to the cross-examination of witnesses.

PROSECUTOR: I stand corrected, M'Lord.

JUDGE: It is completely unnecessary for you to hammer home such patently obvious points to seventy-two of the most learned gentlemen in the Province. We have all heard the testimony, and there cannot be the slightest grounds for doubt in our minds as to its accuracy and concurrence.

PROSECUTOR: Thank you very much,' M'Lord. In that case, I shall not burden the court with any further witnesses on this parti-cular charge.

JUDGE: I suppose the prisoner still has no questions?

CLERK: Prisoner, have you any questions of these witnesses?

CLERK: As usual, no questions.

PROSECUTOR: I would like to call Reverend Matthat Ben Hezron.

CLERK: Call the Reverend Matthat Ben Hezron. (*He is sworn.*)

PROSECUTOR: Reverend Hezron, are you a loyal subject of Caesar?

WITNESS: Oh indeed I am. I always pay my taxes.

PROSECUTOR: And have you ever discussed Ceasar's taxes with the prisoner you see there?

WITNESS: Very much so. We showed him a coin bearing the graven image and inscription of Tiberius and asked him what he thought of it as regards the First and Second Commandment. Was it lawful, we asked, for devout Jews to pay Caesar with idolatrous coins?

PROSECUTOR: And how did prisoner respond?

WITNESS: He indicated we should not.

PROSECUTOR: You mean he told you to withhold your lawful tribute from Caesar?

WITNESS: Yes, he said we should not give tribute to Caesar.

PROSECUTOR: Incitement to withhold taxes!

JUDGE: What were his exact words?

WITNESS: Oh, I can't remember exactly. But that's what he implied.

PROSECUTOR: Thank you very much.

VOICE: I can remember.

PROSECUTOR: Who . . .?

ELDER: Nicodemus, Elder of this Grand Council now in session. I speak as of my rights.

PROSECUTOR: Pray do, your Lordship.

ELDER: I recall his exact words. We had set this question as a deliberate trap. So we did not forget in a hurry. He said: "Render unto Caesar the things that are Caesar's and to God the things that are God's."

WITNESS: That was nothing like it. I took a note at the time.

ELDER: Then why can't you remember?

JUDGE: In any case, it seems a most equivocal answer.

ELDER: A very good answer in my opinion. (*Interruptions.*)

CLERK: Silence! Silence!

JUDGE: Reverend my Lords, apart from our brother Nicodemus, do any of you who were present on that occasion have any doubts in your minds that prisoner's remarks were seditious and unlawful and directed against Caesar, his crown and dignity? Speak up: (*Silence.*)

JUDGE: I'm afraid, Nicodemus, you are overruled by a majority of seventy-one in addition to this witness.

PROSECUTOR: Well, that seems very clear, so now I should like the court's leave to present . . .

ELDER: No, it doesn't!

PROSECUTOR: As I was saying, I should like leave to present evidence concerning the obstruction of justice, to wit, prevention of the execution by lawful authorities of a female person sentenced under the relevant sections: "Adulterous Females, Stoning of; in accordance with the Law of Moses." My first witness is a worthy Pharisee, Barnabas Ben Achiab, by name.

CLERK: Call Barnabas Ben Achiab. (*He is sworn.*)

PROSECUTOR: Are you a Pharisee?

WITNESS: I have that distinction.

PROSECUTOR: Had you any special function regarding the prisoner you see here before the court?

WITNESS: Yes, sir, I had.

PROSECUTOR: And what was that function?

WITNESS: Like the previous witness, I too had undertaken to be one who is called a "Provocative Agent". I had been assigned to put a test question to the prisoner in an attempt to discover his religious credentials.

PROSECUTOR: And by what authority were you given this assignment?

WITNESS: By the Intelligence Division of the Grand Council of the Sanhedrin.

PROSECUTOR: Very good. And did you put your test question to the prisoner?

WITNESS: I did.

PROSECUTOR: Describe the circumstances.

WITNESS: We'd convicted a woman of adultery.

PROSECUTOR: Oh yes?

WITNESS: And we brought her to the customary place for stoning at a time we knew prisoner would be present. To put him to the test, we explained the charges and emphasized the fact that the guilty party had admitted to them in full confession and in minute detail – Shall I quote the details?

JUDGE: I think we can dispose with squalid details. (*Murmurs.*)

CLERK: Silence! Silence in court!

WITNESS: So we said to prisoner: Moses, in his law, prescribed that such persons be stoned to death. But how about you? What is your sentence?

PROSECUTOR: I see. Hoping to catch him out?

WITNESS: Exactly.

PROSECUTOR: And what was his reply?

WITNESS: Nothing, at first. He bent down and began writing on the ground with his finger – so we kept on repeating the question till he was willing to give us a civil answer?

PROSECUTOR: And did he?

WITNESS: In due course. But it was hardly civil.

PROSECUTOR: In what way?

WITNESS: He picked up one of the stones prepared for the execution, as if weighing it in his hand. Then he turned and looked at each and every one of us, and had the audacity to say: "Whichever of you is free from sin shall cast the first stone." Then he held out the stone to see who would take it.

PROSECUTOR: There were many takers, no doubt?

WITNESS: Er – no sir.

PROSECUTOR: Not *one*?

WITNESS: No . . .

PROSECUTOR: Oh come, come, not a single taker? (Witness indicates a negative answer)

PROSECUTOR: Not even *you*?

JUDGE: Witness need not answer that question.

WITNESS: Thank you, Your Grace.

PROSECUTOR: Then I put it to you in another way. After this singular, and apparently universal, reluctance towards stone-throwing, what did you do next?

WITNESS: Well, as I said, he bent down and went on writing on the ground with his finger.

PROSECUTOR: I didn't ask you what *he* did. I asked what *you* did.

WITNESS: Well, we er – we all went away, but the Elders went first!

PROSECUTOR: You all slunk away?

WITNESS: Well, we left. There didn't seem to be much point in staying.

PROSECUTOR: You *slunk* away?

WITNESS: I suppose you might call it that.

PROSECUTOR: How very edifying. The entire assemblage of officials – scribes and pharisees, priests and doctors, so demoralized by the insinuations (unfounded, naturally!) of a single rebellious agitator, that they slink off into the shadows, leaving a convicted sinner unpunished.

WITNESS: Oh but I was the first to come back, and I caught him alone with this adulterous woman.

PROSECUTOR: Most interesting. And what, pray, took place when you found him alone with this adulterous woman?

WITNESS: He finished off his writing and looked up as if surprised to see they'd all gone. "Woman," he said; "where are your accusers? Has no one condemned you?" "No one, Lord," she said. And he said to her: "Then neither will I condemn you. Go your way and sin no more."

PROSECUTOR: What then?

WITNESS: He started into us with a lecture. He said: "I am the Light of the World. He who follows me can never walk in darkness. He will possess the light which is life." So we said to him: "Look here, you're testifying on your own behalf which is worth nothing!" So he answered back: "My testimony is trustworthy, even when I testify on my own behalf. I know where I've come from and I know where I'm going. You set yourself up to judge after your earthly fashion. I do not set myself up to judge anybody. And what if I should judge? My judgement is judgement indeed, for it is not I alone, but my Father who sent me."

PROSECUTOR: More of this messianic delusion, I see. Can you tell the court, by any chance, what the prisoner wrote on the ground with his finger?

WITNESS: Must I?

JUDGE: There is no need to embarrass witness further, he need not answer the question.

WITNESS: *Thank you*, Your Grace.

PROSECUTOR: Then I have no more questions. Call the next witness.

CLERK: He is not present.

PROSECUTOR: Then call the following witness.

CLERK: He is not here either.

PROSECUTOR: But I subpoenaed at least a dozen witnesses to this event. They must be here!

CLERK: I'm very sorry, sir. But there are none of them present.

JUDGE: Very distressing for you learned counsel.

PROSECUTOR: My Lord, this is outrageous! There is ample corroborative testimony to the charge.

JUDGE: Then where is it? Where are they? By the way, your junior counsel seems to be making frantic signals, perhaps you should see what he wants?

PROSECUTOR: My junior has just informed me that all the other witnesses to this charge have pleaded to be excused.

JUDGE: On grounds of ill health, I assume?

JUNIOR: Yes, may it please, My Lord. They have all sent medical certificates.

JUDGE: They usually do. I imagine they would take that elementary precaution.

PROSECUTOR: My Lord, I ask that these certificates be investigated and if there is the slightest case of irregularity the offenders be held in contempt of court.

JUDGE: Don't you think you might be rather flogging a dead camel on this count, Learned Counsel? Might you not do better to concentrate on the more serious charges upon which doubtless a plethora of eager witnesses await your questioning?

PROSECUTOR: If My Lord so instructs me.

JUDGE: I merely suggest. It is getting late, and we have barely approached the serious body of evidence.

PROSECUTOR: I shall act upon My Lord's suggestion and proceed to the next charge. Call Dr Elezaar Ben Zacharias.

CLERK: Call Dr Elezaar Ben Zacharias. (*He is sworn.*)

PROSECUTOR: Doctor Zacharias, are you a doctor of medicine?

WITNESS: Yes, sir, twenty-five years in private practice. I have my surgery in Capernaum where I was attending the son of a titled gentleman who was very seriously ill. Now, my noble patient's father heard this so-called miracle worker was in the district – at Cana to be precise – and paid me the very dubious honour of calling the prisoner here for a second opinion.

JUDGE: Cana? Cana? Isn't that where he was meant to have produced a lot of wine at some wedding – very good wine too, from all accounts?

WITNESS: I believe it was. Anyway, my patient's father –

JUDGE: Without a vintner's licence?

PROSECUTOR: I imagine that goes without saying.

JUDGE: A civil offence, not within the jurisdiction of this court. Pray continue, Doctor.

WITNESS: Well, at first the prisoner was reluctant to come. He told my patient's father: "You only believe when you see signs and miracles." But my lord entreated him: "Please come home with me and heal my son. He is on the point of death."

PROSECUTOR: And how did prisoner respond? Did he go with him?

WITNESS: No, he didn't. He said: "Go back home. Your son will live."

PROSECUTOR: Did he?

WITNESS: He got better at the same hour.

PROSECUTOR: What time was that?

WITNESS: About the seventh hour.

PROSECUTOR: And at what time did the fever break?

WITNESS: At the seventh hour; pure coincidence, of course.

PROSECUTOR: Or, faith healing?

WITNESS: How could it be faith healing, my patient knew nothing about it? Never even met the prisoner. No, it was sheer coincidence.

PROSECUTOR: But when his father returned, he found his son alive and well?

WITNESS: Yes.

PROSECUTOR: How very inconclusive. Call the next witness.

CLERK: A leper, M'Lud. I hasten to add he is cleansed and has his temple Certificate of Cleansing with him.

JUDGE: I should hope so. Let me see the certificate – seems in order. But I should like to question the priest who issued this certificate in my chambers. (*Witness is sworn.*)

PROSECUTOR: Now, then, leper – I *beg* your pardon – *ex*-leper. Tell my lords here exactly what happened to you.

WITNESS: Well, sir, when I heard of all the wonderful things he was doing I prayed and prayed I might find him and be made whole. Then, sir, one wonderful day he came along and I knelt at his feet and I begged him: "Master, if it be your will, you have power to make me clean." Then I looked up and I saw tears of pity in his eyes. And he stretched out his hand and said: "It is my will that you be made clean." And I *was* . . . just like that. I was made clean and whole!

PROSECUTOR: You addressed him as "Master" you say. By what right –

WITNESS: Oh, he's a Master sure enough. Only a Master, a real Master, a great great Master, could do what he did to me.

JUDGE: Witness will not venture private opinions.

PROSECUTOR: Thank you, M'Lord! Have you, ex-leper, anything more to tell the court?

WITNESS: Only that he said: "Go and show yourself to the priest and offer the gift for your cleansing which Moses ordered."

PROSECUTOR: So you ran along and showed yourself to the priest and got your little certificate, and now here you are all nice and whole and clean?

WITNESS: (to Prisoner) I'm sorry, Master: I know I shouldn't have spread the story around like you said. I only came here because I wanted to help you. I hope I haven't done anything wrong?

JUDGE: Witness will cease addressing the prisoner and will stand down. Clerk of the Court, get me the name of the priest who signed his certificate.

CLERK: M'Lud!

PROSECUTOR: There are about nine more ex-lepers. Call the first of them.

CLERK: I'm afraid there's been some confusion M'Lud.

JUDGE: Confusion? There's too much confusion in this case. What's happened now?

CLERK: Well, with the date of the hearing pushed forward and all the many witnesses to be found it's not easy –

JUDGE: Just tell the court what has happened.

CLERK: The witnesses came, M'Lud, but they've had their certificates of cleansing impounded for scrutiny, which means they are unable to enter the court.

JUDGE: Are they outside?

CLERK: No, M'Lud. They had to be sent away. Without their certificates they couldn't possibly stay here. It's in the rules.

JUDGE: I am well aware what is in the rules, Clerk of the Court!

CLERK: But there's another witness from Capernaum, if it please your lordship?

JUDGE: Do you want to call this witness?

PROSECUTOR: If he's here, I do.

CLERK: Call the Rev. Mathias Ben Ishmael. (*He is sworn.*)

PROSECUTOR: Now, good Rabbi, have you ever seen the prisoner before?

WITNESS: Yes, at Capernaum.

PROSECUTOR: Did you ever see him conduct one of his so-called healing miracles at Capernaum.

WITNESS: Yes.

PROSECUTOR: Did you see a certain nobleman's son saved from the point of death?

WITNESS: No. But I heard all about it. It was the talk of the town.

PROSECUTOR: I'm sure it was. But you didn't see it happen?

WITNESS: No, but I saw him casting out devils.

PROSECUTOR: How interesting. Please give us some details.

WITNESS: It was in the synagogue.

PROSECUTOR: In the synagogue at Capernaum, on the Sabbath?

WITNESS: Where else would we be but in the synagogue? It was on the Sabbath and the prisoner was holding forth as if he had some sort of authority. Never once did he look at the Holy Books, but talked as if he understood the inner meaning of the Law better than any of us. This caused somewhat of a commotion, and a man possessed of an evil spirit began to have a fit, kicked and screamed and shouted: "Why do you meddle with us, Jesus of Nazareth? I recognize you for what you are – the Holy One of God."

PROSECUTOR: Did he say that, or the demon within him?

WITNESS: Oh, the demon, no doubt about it. The prisoner's presence was causing him great discomfort.

PROSECUTOR: Or possibly another example of the cunning wiles of the Evil One trying to deceive the Faithful?

WITNESS: Yes, that is it of course. The devil trying to mislead us. But that wasn't the end of it. Oh no! Not by any manner of means. Prisoner spoke to him threateningly: "Silence!" he cried. "Come out of him." Then the possessed threw himself around in the most dreadful contortions and convulsions and the demon came out of him screaming. After that the poor fellow was all right.

PROSECUTOR: Then you do, do you not, consider the prisoner had power over this unclean spirit? Or would you, in your considered opinion, say that prisoner and devil were in league with one another, putting on a show to deceive and mislead?

WITNESS: Well, we Elders were all absolutely astonished – flabbergasted. "What can this be?" we asked ourselves. "What is this marvellous new teaching? See how he has authority to lay his commands even on the unclean spirits!"

INTERRUPTION: Rubbish! They were in cahoots! He was possessed of an evil spirit himself!

JUDGE: If you have anything to put properly before this court take the stand and be sworn.

INTERRUPTION: I will, I will! Just let me have my say!

JUDGE: Thank you. Rabbi. You may go. (*Witness is sworn.*)

PROSECUTOR: What is your name?

WITNESS: Uzziah Ben Nahum, Elder of the synagogue of Capernaum.

PROSECUTOR: So you too were witness to this collusion with devils?

JUDGE: Leading question!

PROSECUTOR: Then I put it this way. Have you seen prisoner cast out, or appear to cast out, devils?

WITNESS: Yes, I saw him cast out a devil from a man who was dumb, and the man spoke. But we knew what he was up to and we called his bluff. We said "You are casting out devils through Beelzebub, the prince of devils. You can't fool us."

PROSECUTOR: What made you so certain?

WITNESS: Because the Lord rests on the Sabbath day and does no work. The only ones who work on the Sabbath Day are evildoers and evil spirits. Therefore if an evil spirit was cast out on the Sabbath day it could only have been through a greater evil spirit – Beelzebub himself!

PROSECUTOR: Your reasoning is impeccable. I could not have put it more lucidly myself.

WITNESS: Thank you, sir.

PROSECUTOR: Will you tell my Lords how prisoner reacted to this very perspicacious observation?

WITNESS: To this what?

JUDGE: What did prisoner do next?

WITNESS: Oh, he was most insolent. He said: "No kingdom can be at war with itself without being destroyed. So how do you imagine Satan's Kingdom can stand firm if it be at war with itself? If it is through Beelzebub I cast out devils, by what means do your own sons cast them out? But if when I cast out devils I do it through God's power, then it must mean that the Kingdom of God has suddenly appeared among you."

PROSECUTION: Did he, indeed?

JUDGE: Has anyone noticed the sudden appearance of God's Kingdom recently – in this court for instance? (*Laughter.*)

INTERRUPTION: Yes, I have!

JUDGE: Silence! Have that man removed.

INTERRUPTION: I wish to testify and testify I shall!

JUDGE: Who is it?

CLERK: A ranking Roman Officer, M'Lud.

INTERRUPTION: P. Caius Marcellus, Centurion of the Imperial Army, Twelfth Legion! I demand the right to speak in this court without let or hindrance. I'm going to put some of you people right!

JUDGE: But of course, of course, good sir. We are all Caesar's friends. It is very good of you to trouble yourself with our purely internal matters. Pray take the Oath – the *Roman* Oath, Clerk! Not the Torah, you fool! (*He is sworn on the Roman Oath.*)

WITNESS: Now, you lot, just listen to me!

PROSECUTOR: What is your name and rank?

WITNESS: I've already told you, so will you stop interrupting and let me get on with it? Thank you. Right! Now I'll tell you a thing or two about the Kingdom of God. I've seen it at close quarters. It's not that I'm a very religious man: Jove, Jehovah, it's all the same to me. But I know there's some kind of Goodness looking after us all, whatever our race or religion, because I've had it happen to me.

All right, I'm not even a Jew. To you I'm a gentile, a bloody heretic and infidel. But that didn't seem to make much odds with your Prophet here. He doesn't give a hoot what you are, or what your race, creed and class. Anyone who needs help, just go and ask him for it, they said. So I did. I asked him for help and he gave it. Now, I have an orderly who's been with me through every campaign. Splendid fellow! Love him like my own son – would give his life for me if he had to! Well anyway, this dear fellow took badly sick and was dying. M.O. couldn't do a thing for him. Gave him up for lost. Well, I've always stuck up for you colonials, treated you the same as I'd treat a Roman citizen. I've dozens of Jewish friends. Ask them if you don't believe me. I even put up the cash for the new Capernaum synagogue. So I sent some of your Elders to go out and find this Jesus and ask him to come and try and do something.

So my good Jewish friends hurry off and beg the kind Jesus to come and save my poor orderly. But I can't bear sitting around doing nothing, so after they'd gone I rode out after them, and was absolutely thrilled to see them returning with the holy Prophet. Made me feel a bit of a chump, really. I mean, who was I, a mere soldier, a Roman, to go making demands on the Son of your God? So when I met him I said to him: "Dear Lord, please don't trouble yourself to come all the way back to my house because I am not worthy that you should even enter my door. But just give the command and I know my servant will be healed. You see, Lord, I know what it is to give orders. I say to my chaps, Go, and they go, Come and they come, at the double too! So just give the word and my orderly will be right as rain."

JUDGE: Pray continue, Noble Roman!

CENTURION: It worked, of course. Never doubted it wouldn't. Not for one minute! Pretty marvellous really! He even said some very nice things about me believing in him. Now listen to me, High Priest! I have to return to duty now, but if I hear you've so much as harmed a hair of this dear good man's head I'll see you get kicked out of that office of yours and lose every perk you've ever had. I have a little influence with the Governor General you know and I shall use it! I mean that!

JUDGE: Thank you for coming, Noble Roman! (*Witness leaves amid interruptions.*)

JUDGE: Are there any more foreigners who wish to testify against the State?

CLERK: No, M'Lud.

JUDGE: What about Martha and Mary of Bethany? Didn't the prisoner raise their brother from the dead? Surely they'd like to give evidence on his behalf?

CLERK: They are not in court.

JUDGE: I have a particular interest in this case. I was hoping we might have some witnesses to it? Come, come, Bethany isn't very far, surely there's someone?

CLERK: There's a witness here, M'Lord, a man from the neighbourhood of Bethany. (*He is sworn.*)

PROSECUTOR: What is your name?

WITNESS: Joshua Ben Mattathias. I knew this Lazarus and I remember when he died. We all went out to comfort Martha and

Mary who were very upset. Jesus hadn't been there, for they thought he'd have saved him from dying if he'd been present. Anyway, by the time he arrived, Lazarus had been buried four days, so Jesus tried to comfort the family, saying he would rise again. And Martha said: "I know he'll rise again at the Resurrection," and Jesus said: "I am the Resurrection and the life. He who believes in me though he is dead, shall live forever."

JUDGE: I want to make a note of that.

WITNESS: She said: "Yes, Lord, I believe this. I have come to believe that you are the Christ, you are the Son of the Living God, and the world has waited for you to come."

JUDGE: The Court will take note of this.

WITNESS: Well, poor Mary was in tears, and everyone around was in tears, and when he saw it, Jesus was deeply upset, and sighed deeply. Then he suddenly turned and asked: "Where have you buried him?" And they said: "Come and see." And as they set off through the graveyard Jesus began to weep and sob. And they all said: "Look how he loved him. Couldn't he, who opened blind men's eyes, have prevented this man's death?" And Jesus, still crying, came to the cave which was Lazarus's tomb. The stone lid had been put on the grave, but Jesus wiped away his tears and said: "Take away the stone!" "But Lord," Martha said, "he's been in there four days now and the air will be foul!" And Jesus, turned to her, very kind and gentle, and said: "But dear Martha, haven't I told you that if you have Faith, you will see God glorified?" So they got the stone out of the way, and Jesus suddenly straightened himself up and lifted his face up to heaven: "Father, thank you! thank you! thank you for hearing my prayer! For myself I know you hear me at all times. But I say this now for the sake of all these people standing round, so they may learn to believe that it is *you* who have sent me and it is *you* who do these marvellous works through me."

Then he called out in a very loud voice: "Lazarus! Come out! Come to my side!" And to our amazement the dead man came staggering out, all wound up in the funeral shrouds; his face muffled in the veil. And Jesus – oh he was radiant – he said, "Come on! get him out of his wrappings and let him go free."

JUDGE: Thank you, you may stand down. Step up here please, Learned Counsel.

PROSECUTOR: Certainly, M'Lord.

JUDGE: (*Privately to Prosecutor*): This was the case I told you about which caused us to hold a special meeting of the Council. We were extremely concerned that if things were allowed to continue like this, our Noble Occupiers would carry out their oft repeated threats to put an end to our race and our city as a final solution to their problem. I went on record as saying they had absolutely no foresight. I could clearly see that the validity or otherwise of this man's works were quite irrelevant. So I said, do you not feel that it is best for us if one man has to be put to death for the sake of our people, and save the whole nation from a pogrom? One doesn't terribly enjoy having to make these kind of decisions. But it's a question of choosing the lesser evil. Agree?

PROSECUTOR: Agree!

JUDGE: Then you realize how imperative it is to secure a conviction; not only here, but a conviction that will stand up in the Supreme Court?

PROSECUTOR: My Lord, you are born of wisdom.

JUDGE: So would you like, perhaps, to call a witness concerning the charge of practising medicine and healing on the Sabbath Day?

PROSECUTOR: That might expedite my case.

JUDGE: Then the Clerk will call the man who was born blind and was healed of his blindness-from-birth.

PROSECUTOR: With respect, my Lord!

JUDGE: I beg your pardon?

PROSECUTOR: My Lord, it is not yet proven that this witness was blind as from birth. It is only his statement that leads us so to believe.

JUDGE: It says here: "A man, who was born blind."

PROSECUTOR: Then with respect I ask the Courts leave to correct it to re-read: "A man who *claimed* to have been blind as from birth."

JUDGE: Really, Learned Counsel, this is very pernickety. I honestly fail to see the difference!

PROSECUTOR: With very great respect, My Lord, there is a considerable difference. I need hardly be so presumptuous as to point out to so eminent a theologian as Your Grace the doctrine regarding the relationship of illness to sin.

JUDGE: Oh, I see what you're driving at. Very well, for the record let him be known as the man, *said* to have been born blind.

And for the benefit of any Reverend Member of the Counsel who's theology has become dim with time, I shall remind him briefly of the Doctrine of the Holy Jewish Church on the relationship of sickness to sin. Sickness is the direct punishment by God for sin. A man who has never sinned is never ill. Sickness of the body is but a reflection of sickness of the soul. Therefore a man cannot truly be healed until his sins are forgiven him. I think that is the point Learned Counsel wishes to be brought home – that the Church teaches that a man is blind because he has done something deserving of blindness. But if he be *born* blind, as opposed to *going* blind, then it is held that he is either paying for some unexpiated transgressions of his parents, or (according to some schools of thought) his misfortune is held to be the result of crimes committed in a previous existence. In either case, Learned Counsel is trying to show that if the witness you are about to hear was not born blind, but suffered blindness as a *result* of present sin, then this fact must be taken into account in assessing his character and validity as a witness.

PROSECUTOR: My Lord could not have been more explicit.

JUDGE: Thank you – my remarks should also be borne in mind if we have to do with prisoner's alleged forgiveness of sins at the time of alleged healings. So, now, call this man who was blind.

CLERK: Call the man who was blind.

JUDGE: What *is* that thing? Clerk of the Court why are you waving that piece of stuff about – what is it?

CLERK: Evidence, M'Lud.

JUDGE: Evidence of what, pray?

CLERK. Of one of his followers, M'Lud, the accused's followers.

JUDGE: What on earth are you talking about?

CLERK: It was the young man, sir, the young man who was with him at the time of the arrest, the young man in a white garment.

JUDGE: Well, he doesn't seem to be in it now, does he?

CLERK: No, M'Lud. He slipped out of it when they grabbed him. Ran off all naked he did.

JUDGE: Then let us hope he doesn't catch cold. (*Laughter.*) Now stop flapping that thing around! And stop interrupting me!

CLERK: Sorry, M'Lud.

PROSECUTOR: Are you the man who was healed of blindness on the Sabbath Day?

WITNESS: Aye, sir, I was.

PROSECUTOR: You can see now all right, your eyesight has perfectly recovered?

WITNESS: Oh yes! Thanks be to the great and merciful God!

PROSECUTOR: Then, can you see in this court the man you say healed you on that Sabbath Day?

WITNESS: You want me to point him out?

PROSECUTOR: Point him out to Their Lordships.

WITNESS: Why, has he done something wrong? You're not going to hurt him – are you?

PROSECUTOR: You're not here to ask questions just do as you're told.

WITNESS: It was – it was him – Dear Master I never thanked you enough. Anything I can do or say . . .

JUDGE: You will not address the prisoner. You will only answer questions, or I shall hold you in contempt.

PROSECUTOR: After this touching little demonstration will you tell the Court in your own words the events leading up to, and the events following, your remarkable cure?

WITNESS: Most gladly I will, sir. I shall never forget it.

PROSECUTOR: Continue!

WITNESS: Well I heard all these people coming past me, and one says to another: "Master what has this man done that he be born blind?"

JUDGE: You were definitely *born* blind?

WITNESS: Oh yes, My Lord. Blind from birth. Couldn't see a thing.

JUDGE: Carry on.

WITNESS: And this man says: Did he do something bad or did his Mum and Dad? And this other one – Master over there – says: "Neither he nor his parents were guilty. He was born blind so that God's glory might manifest itself in him."

PROSECUTOR: Have you the faintest idea what that was meant to mean?

WITNESS: Yes, sir. Funnily enough I think I have. Well anyway, suddenly he spits and makes some clay into a paste and sticks it on my eyes and tells me "Away with you and wash in the Pool of Siloe." So off I goes and washes like he says, and it happens! I'm cured! I can see! And he did it! Master over there did it, God bless and love him for it!

JUDGE: If you were blind when it happened, how are you now able to recognize him?

WITNESS: I was coming to that. I never saw him again for a while. I wanted to thank him, naturally enough, but he'd just gone away and vanished; left the area. Well then there was no end of a rumpus. No one could believe it. Even my neighbours said it wasn't me, but someone who looked like me. And then the police hauled me up before these Pharisees and I told them what I told you, and they carried on about it being on the Sabbath Day, as if it was something wrong to see God's glory on the Sabbath Day.

PROSECUTOR: Will the Court note witness's insistence that it *was* the Sabbath Day!

WITNESS: Look, all I know is I was blind, and now I can see! I don't know anything about any Sabbath Days! If you'd never seen the sun, and then you do see it, you'd not go around asking what day of week it was.

PROSECUTOR: But you would agree, would you not, that a man who breaks the Sabbath is a sinner?

WITNESS: Yeah, that's what all these Pharisees and other gentlemen kept on about. How can a sinner heal a blind man, they says. Kept on arguing and arguing. Made my head spin.

PROSECUTOR: And what do you think your benefactor was?

WITNESS: Like I said at the police station – he's a Prophet! What else?

JUDGE: That is a private opinion.

WITNESS: Well, he must be, mustn't he? I mean to say—

PROSECUTOR: What had your good parents to make of all this?

WITNESS: Oh them? They was proper scared.

PROSECUTOR: On what grounds?

WITNESS: Well, they never let up, never for one moment.

PROSECUTOR: Who never let up?

WITNESS: All these investigators, doctors, Pharisees or whatever they was, got poor old Mum scared, proper scared. Got her so she was afraid to answer any more questions. So Mum just says: "Look we don't know who done it. Honest we don't. Ask our boy. He's over twenty-one. Let him tell you his own story."

PROSECUTOR: Oh come now, surely no one was trying to intimidate your good mother?

WITNESS: Oh yes they was! They let it get around that anyone who even hinted this Jesus was the Christ was going to get slung out of the synagogue, and my people's good churchgoers, never miss a Sabbath. They was in a blue funk they was going to get excommunicated.

PROSECUTOR: And were they?

WITNESS: No. They shut up about it. Wouldn't say a word.

PROSECUTOR: Were *you*?

WITNESS: Was I what?

PROSECUTOR: Were you excommunicated?

WITNESS: Yes, and it was a crying shame. I never done nothing. I only told the truth I only –

JUDGE: Court will note we are dealing with an excommunicant.

PROSECUTOR: And what happened after that?

WITNESS: They kept hauling me back to the police station and going over it again and again and again. They says not to give praise to this man who'd done it. "Give praise to God", they says, "This man to our knowledge is a sinner." "I don't know about that", I says. "All I know is I was born blind and couldn't see. But now I can see. What more do you want?"

Then they starts up again: "What was it he did to you? How did he make you see? What methods did he use?" There was this doctor fellow. Very posh. All sorts of degrees, five pieces of silver a minute just to talk to him. So I tells him for the umpteenth time that He just spat in the mud and plastered it over my eyes and then sent me off to the pool to wash. That's all. I told them, and I'm telling you. But they wouldn't believe a word of it. . . . Do . . . you believe me?

PROSECUTOR: Possibly. But just so the Court has no lingering doubts I'd like you to repeat your story – a little more concisely if possible.

WITNESS: Why do you want it all over again? Are you thinking of becoming his disciples?

JUDGE: Don't you dare address Learned Counsel like that! You worthless common, lying, stupid little oaf! You will keep your discipleship to yourself. We are here disciples of Moses. Any more quips like that and I'll have you flogged for contempt of Court.

WITNESS: Begging the Court's pardon, I'm all confused. I mean it's pretty marvellous isn't it? Like I said before, when they hauled

68

me in for more questioning, I said, here's this man. Where he comes from, where he's gone, no one knows. But we know for certain that God spoke to Moses. But we know nothing of this man or where he's come from, but he's made me see. Now, we know for certain that the Good God doesn't answer sinners' prayers. It's only these people what's devout and do his will that gets their prayers answered. So, for a sinner like me, born blind and then cured is something no one's ever heard of since the world began! So I says to them "If this man who cured me did not come from God, he wouldn't have no powers at all, would he?"

JUDGE: Quite a little theologian, aren't we! Do you really expect us to take lessons in divinity from a wretch like you, by your very own admission – steeped in sin from birth?

WITNESS: That's what they all said when they excommunicated me. They only did it because I wouldn't tell lies and get him into trouble. But I couldn't do that, could I, not to the Son of God?

PROSECUTOR: To the *what*?

WITNESS: The Son of God – Him over there.

JUDGE: Strike that from the record!

WITNESS: But I saw him. I was out wandering around on the city dump when I saw him again. I'd been searching everywhere for him. Wanted to thank him and tell him how good God was when I suddenly see Him coming to look for me – How d'yer like that? *He* comes looking for *me*? "Do you believe in the Son of God?" he says. "Dear Lord" I says: "Tell me who he is so I can believe in him."

Then he says – it was marvellous, I'll never forget it, long as I live! – He says: "He is the One you have seen. It is He who is speaking to you." And I felt me knees go all funny. It's like a big light inside me and all around me and I fell down on my knees and worshipped him – (*Witness is overcome with emotion and unable to continue.*)

PROSECUTOR: I think we have heard quite enough from you my man! Will you rule him to be a Hostile Witness, M'Lord?

JUDGE: I shall. The Court may disregard the latter part of his testimony, but will note that, by his own admission, he was a sinner and quite properly excommunicated. Witness may stand down unless, of course, the prisoner has any questions – no questions? – not even of a witness so patently biased on your behalf?

CLERK: No questions, M'Lud.

JUDGE: Prisoner will not smile at witness like that, unless he wishes to betray their obvious collusion. Guards will assist witness to his feet and remove him from my court!

CLERK: Prisoner appears to have something to say, M'Lud.

JUDGE: Has he, indeed? And about time too!

PRISONER: I have come into this world so that a sentence may fall upon it, that those who are blind should see, and that those who think they can see should become blind.

PROSECUTOR: Oh, are we blind too?

PRISONER: If you were blind you would not suffer from guilt. It is because you protest: "We can see so clearly," that you cannot rid yourself of guilt.

JUDGE: Prisoner will refrain from impertinent remarks. But perhaps he will offer some explanation for the slanders, calumnies and threats uttered against the Elders and Rulers of the Temple, against the Scribes and Pharisees and against our most holy Office? Let us see what answer he has to Scribe Nicodemus Ben Jacob. Call him!

CLERK: Call Scribe Nicodemus Ben Jacob! (*He is sworn.*)

PROSECUTOR: Good Scribe, have you ever seen the prisoner before?

WITNESS: Yes, sir, on several occasions.

PROSECUTOR: Was any one of those several occasions very outstanding?

WITNESS: Outstanding? It was *un*believable!

JUDGE: Tell us about it.

WITNESS: May it please your Lordship. It was at a dinner party given by my very good friend Joshua Ben Ames, a Pharisee of impeccable manners who had very kindly included the prisoner in his guest list. My host was most embarrassed when prisoner came to table without the correct ritual washing.

PROSECUTOR: Not washing?

WITNESS: Not even his hands!

PROSECUTOR: Disgusting!

WITNESS: No decent Jew would dream of sitting down to dine without the full ritual wash and brush-up as laid down by law. I said to myself, this man's behaving like an atheist. Of course my host was very put out. When he raised his eyebrows and asked if he would care to visit the men's room, prisoner was rather rude.

PROSECUTOR: What did he say?

WITNESS: Something very coarse. Something to the effect that things you eat don't make you dirty. Anything you eat goes through your belly and out into the drains. What makes a man dirty, he said, is the dirt that comes out of his heart and out of his mouth.

PROSECUTOR: What a very boorish way to treat his host!

WITNESS: The party was completely ruined. But there was no stopping him. He picked up the tableware, all clean and sparkling in his unwashed hands, and began a long seditious and slanderous speech against the religious authorities. Now I'm a scribe of no mean ability. Fifty words a minute, and I'm able to memorize long dictations and set them down days later. I pride myself on the accuracy of my work –

JUDGE: Yes, yes, yes.

WITNESS: I was so appalled I set down his whole slanderous speech, if only as a warning to gentlemen as to who they ask to their dinners. I've got it here. Shall I read it out? Oh! –

JUDGE: Will the Usher kindly help him pick up his scrolls?

WITNESS: Thank you, sir – now let me see. Ah yes. Now – just listen to what he had to say about us – and about Your Grace's Holy Office. He said: "The Scribes and The Pharisees" (that's us) "have established themselves in the place which Moses used to teach. Do what they tell you then. Continue to observe what they tell you, but do *not* imitate their actions. For they tell you one thing and do another. They fasten up packs too heavy to be borne, and lay them on men's shoulders, but they themselves will not stir a finger to lift them."

JUDGE: Since when has the Most Honourable Company of Scribes been required to act like common labourers?

WITNESS: Exactly, My Lord. Then he added further insult: "They act, always, so as to be a mark for men's eyes. Boldly written are the texts they carry, and deep is the hem of their garments. Their heart is set on taking the best places at table and the first seats in the synagogue, and having their hands kissed in the market place, and being called Rabbi among their fellow men." Then he said to his followers: "You are not to claim the title of Rabbi. You have but one Master, and you are all brethren alike. Nor are you to call any man on earth your father. You have but one Father and He is in heaven."

71

PROSECUTOR: It helps to know who one's father is. I understand there is a certain doubt in the case of the so-called carpenter's son.

JUDGE: Proceed!

WITNESS: "Nor are you to be called teachers. You have one teacher – Christ."

JUDGE: Did he say "Christ"?

WITNESS: He did, My Lord. Most plainly and audibly.

JUDGE: Carry on while I make a note.

WITNESS: Then came a direct challenge to established society, a complete reversal of our entire social system.

JUDGE: Witness will not venture opinions. He will confine himself to giving evidence.

WITNESS: I stand rebuked. I mean he then went on to say: "Among you, the greatest of all is to be the servant of all –"

JUDGE: I see.

WITNESS: "The man who exalts himself will be humbled and the man who humbles himself will be exalted. Woe upon you, Priests and Lawyers! You hypocrites that slam the door of the kingdom of heaven in men's faces. You will neither enter it yourselves, nor let others enter when they would."

PROSECUTOR: A complete denial of the function of the spiritual authorities!

WITNESS: "Woe upon you, Priests and Lawyers, you hypocrites that swallow up the property of widows under cover of your long prayers. Your sentence will be all the heavier for that."

JUDGE: The Court is doubtless aware that it is perfectly proper to make suitable offerings in return for prayers and supplications. The size of such offerings depending entirely on the sincerity of the donor.

WITNESS: "Woe upon you, Priests and Lawyers, you hypocrites that encompass sea and land to gain a single proselyte, and then make the proselyte twice as worthy of damnation as yourselves. Woe upon you, Blind Leaders, who say: If a man swears by the Temple it goes for nothing. But if he swears by the gold in the Temple his oath stands. Blind fools! Which is the greater, the gold – or the Temple that consecrates the gold?"

PROSECUTOR: Without its gold how could the Temple function?

WITNESS: And again, "If a man swears by the Altar it goes for nothing. But if he swears by the gift on the Altar his oath stands.

Blind fools! Which is the greater – the gift on the Altar, or the Altar that consecrates the gift? The man who swears by the Altar swears at the same time by all that is on it. The man who swears by the Temple swears at the same time by Him who has made it his dwelling place. And the man who swears by heaven swears not only by God's Throne, but by Him who sits upon it."

JUDGE: Any more?

WITNESS: Oh yes, plenty – "Woe upon you, Priests and Lawyers, you hypocrites that will award to God his tithe, though it only be of mint or dill or cumin and have forgotten the weight or commandments of the law – Justice – Mercy – and Honour. You did ill to forget one duty while you performed the other. You blind leaders that have a strainer for the gnat, and then swallow the camel!"

PROSECUTOR: I would say gastronomically impossible. (*Laughter*.)

WITNESS: Then he became really insufferable. Just listen to this: "Woe upon you, Priests and Lawyers, you hypocrites that scour the outward part of cup and dish, while all within is running with avarice and corruption. Scour the inside of cup and dish first, you blind Lawyer, so that the outside, too, may become clean. Woe upon you, Priests and Lawyers, you hypocrites that are like whitened sepulchres, fair in outward appearance, when they are full of dead men's bones and all manner of corruption within. You seem exact over your duties, outwardly to men's eyes, while there is nothing within you but hypocrisy and iniquity. Woe upon you, Priests and Lawyers, you hypocrites that built up the tombs of the prophets and engraved the monuments of the just. You say: if we had lived in our fathers' times we would not have taken part in murdering the prophets. Why then, you bear witness of your own ancestry. It was *your* fathers who slaughtered the prophets. It is for you to complete your fathers' reckoning. Serpents that you are! Brood of vipers! How should you escape from the award of hell? And now, behold, I am sending wise men and men of learning to preach to you."

JUDGE: Did ye say that *he* would send?

WITNESS: He did, My Lord.

JUDGE: I see.

WITNESS: "Men of learning to preach to you," he said. "Some of them you will put to death and crucify. Some you will scourge in your synagogues."

JUDGE: More than likely!

WITNESS: Yes – "and you will persecute them from city to city, so that you will make yourselves answerable for all the blood of just men that is shed on earth, from the blood of the just Abel to the blood of Zacharias the son of Barachias whom you slew between the Temple and the Altar – believe me this generation shall be held answerable for all of it."

JUDGE: Is he threatening the Priesthood? Is he presuming to judge Us, to call Us to account?

WITNESS: Oh undoubtedly. He accused you of murder. (*Consternation.*) Yes, murder. He went on to say: "Jerusalem, Jerusalem, still murdering the prophets and stoning the Messengers that are sent to you. How often have I been ready to gather your children together, as a hen gathers her chicks under her wings, and you refused it? Behold your house is left to you, a house uninhabited. Believe me, you shall see nothing of me henceforward, until the time when you shall be saying: "Blessed is he that comes in the name of the Lord."

PROSECUTOR: My Lord, this is unbelievable. The prisoner is an anarchist and a blasphemer.

JUDGE: He called *us* murderers? Called *us* a brood of vipers!

WITNESS: Exactly as I took it down here.

JUDGE: Prisoner, do you wish to contest any of the evidence you have just heard?

CLERK: Answer, when My Lord addresses you!

JUDGE: Prisoner, you are pursuing a most reckless and dangerous course that can only end in your death and damnation. It is my duty to explain to you, in case you do not fully understand the serious implications of Sections 6 and 7 of the Act. Section 6 states: "The Grand Sanhedrin in the Temple of Jerusalem hands down the law in the name of God. God himself respects these decisions." Now listen carefully: Section 7 — "Defiance of the Grand Sanhedrin's authority shall be punished by death", and Section 8 — "Disobedience to the Grand Sanhedrin's decisions shall be punished by death." And once more in Section 13 (Defiance of the Priests, the Temple, or the Temple Rites): "Whosoever defies the officiating priests in Jerusalem shall die."

So I shall ask you once again, did you in fact speak against priests and elders, the authorities, religious and temporal in the manner described by this witness in evidence? Very well, the court

74

has no alternative but to take your silence as an admission that his evidence is correct. I should like to thank the witness for the detailed and painstaking manner in which he presented his evidence. It *does* help when we have men of your education to testify.

WITNESS: Thank you very much, My Lord.

PROSECUTOR: In view of your lordship's remarks I should like the court to see the dreadful effects prisoner's diatribes can have on anyone foolish enough to take them seriously. I have next a rich young nobleman who has already ruined himself and his family fortunes under the insidious influence of the prisoner and all he stands for.

JUDGE: Then let him speak. (*Witness is sworn.*) Tell the Court your name.

WITNESS: Jonathan Kantheros.

PROSECUTOR: You are very young to be so rich. Did you earn or did you inherit your wealth?

WITNESS: I inherited it. But I'm no longer rich.

PROSECUTOR: Why not?

WITNESS: I gave it all away.

PROSECUTOR: Yet I understand you were what we would term a playboy?

WITNESS: You might. I'd far too much money. Didn't know what to do with it. I kept a number of private carriages. I'd my own pleasure boat on the Mediterranean. I gambled, gave parties – until I met this man Jesus.

PROSECUTOR: Then what happened? Did he con it off you?

JUDGE: Leading question.

PROSECUTOR: Then, did he persuade you to make your fortune over to him by means of a deed of covenant or charitable trust?

WITNESS: No.

PROSECUTOR: Then what did he do?

WITNESS: My money's given me plenty of time for study. I'm not all that much of a playboy. Oh, the parties were fun, and I even enjoyed the hangers-on. If it made them happy to share my wealth, I suppose I kind of enjoyed feeling important. But when I met Jesus I felt a great dissatisfaction in myself. So I asked him: "Master, what must I do to be made perfect?"

PROSECUTOR: Did he suggest you gave it to his party?

WITNESS: No, he said: "If you would be perfect, sell all you have and give it to the poor."

PROSECUTOR: What an incredible idea! Surely you didn't?

WITNESS: It shook me at first. I had a positive trauma! But I did it. I suddenly realized what a damned worry *things* – possessions – can be. Endless taxes, night and day guards on all my possessions, enormous estates, secretaries, servants, dishonest bailiffs and stewards constantly worrying me and distracting from my peace of mind. So one morning I woke up and made a momentous decision. I gave the whole lot to the relief of poverty.

PROSECUTOR: Then how, pray, do you survive? Who buys your food?

WITNESS: We lead a sort of community life. Me and my friends we work and pool everything, we seem to get by all right and we're immensely happy. It's wonderful not to be cluttered up with endless possessions. For the first time in my life I feel free, really free.

PROSECUTOR: Do I take it you're an anarchist?

WITNESS: I have no political leanings. They destroy the soul and clutter the mind every bit as much as too much worldly junk.

PROSECUTOR: You mean you no longer have allegiance to Caesar or to the Jewish authorities?

WITNESS: I didn't say that. We live our lives, do what good we can, but where politics and officials are concerned we observe the laws and mind our own business. You ought to try it one day. Then you wouldn't look so old before your time.

PROSECUTOR: You are being impertinent.

WITNESS: Sorry, it wasn't meant that way. But to me it seems you're wasting your life, bogged down with all these tremendous wordy useless inessentials, when freedom and salvation are staring you in the face.

PROSECUTOR: You are nothing but a social drop-out. You may leave the stand. Here we have a typical example of the kind of disastrous effect the prisoner will have on our economy if he isn't checked.

WITNESS: I wouldn't worry too much if I were you. He's going to have one hell of an effect not only on you but on the whole world before he's done. You'll see!

JUDGE: Witness has left the stand and is no longer in order.

76

JUDGE: Well, reverend gentlemen, if that's a foretaste of what prisoner would have come about, we can all look forward to rags and tatters. Call – (*to Clerk*) Is Jonam Ben Manesseh here? Call him if he is.

CLERK: Call Jonam Ben Manesseh. (*He is sworn.*)

PROSECUTOR: And now a double example of Sabbath breaking, both secular and religious: and some very revealing comments on same by prisoner. Jonam Ben Manesseh, are you an Elder of the Synagogue at Gadara?

WITNESS: I am.

PROSECUTOR: Have you ever seen the prisoner at Gadara on the Sabbath?

WITNESS: Yes, indeed. One Sabbath about the middle of last Tishri we saw his followers walking through the cornfields, plucking off ears of corns and grinding them in their hands to make a meal. So we protested to him: "Look what your disciples are doing. They're breaking the rules!"

PROSECUTOR: How did he reply?

WITNESS: Oh he turned the question round on us.

PROSECUTOR: Yes, he loves doing that!

WITNESS: He asked us if we had read what King David did during the famine, how he entered the House of God at the time when Aliathar was High Priest, and took the Bread of the Presence which only the priests may eat, and gave it out to laymen as a bread ration.

PROSECUTOR: David was a king, and had authority to modify the regulations. This man is a common upstart. His argument is specious and irrelevant.

WITNESS: I agree. And he went on to ask if we'd read in the law how the priests can profane the Sabbath in the Temple without being criticized?

PROSECUTOR: But he is not a priest, nor was he in the Temple.

WITNESS: To hear him talk you'd think he was High Priest and King David rolled into one. He went on to say: "I tell you, there is one standing here who is greater than the Temple. And if you know the meaning of the words: 'I desire mercy not sacrifice', you would not have condemned the innocent." And, as if that weren't enough, he said: "The Sabbath was made for man, not man for the Sabbath!"

77

PROSECUTOR: Disgraceful! He plans to secularize the Holy Day and make his own rules. Would not my Lord agree?

JUDGE: So it would seem.

WITNESS: Anyway, he went back with us to the synagogue, and attended service.

PROSECUTOR: I cannot see why he should bother to attend holy service in view of his previous remarks.

WITNESS: Ah, wait now, wait! We were very glad he did, for there was a man with a withered hand in the congregation and we wanted to see if he'd put his private dispensations into practice. It was almost as if he knew what we were thinking because he immediately told the sick man to come over and stand beside him. Then he looked round at us and asked: "Which of you having an animal fall down a well on the Sabbath will not immediately pull it out? And how much more value is a man than an animal?" Then he said: "I ask you, is it lawful to do good or to do harm on the Sabbath, to save life or to kill?"

PROSECUTOR: Turning the questions round again, I see. I hope you didn't fall into his trap and answer?

WITNESS: No, no, we just kept quiet and let him get on with it.

PROSECUTOR: A wise precaution. How did he react?

WITNESS: He seemed angry – seemed to think we were being heartless. So he said to the sick man: "Stretch out your hand." The man stretched out his withered hand and it suddenly became fit and strong.

PROSECUTOR: You could all testify to that?

WITNESS: Oh yes, we went off and had a discussion with the Herodians, and made affidavits asking that criminal proceedings be instituted against him.

PROSECUTOR: Very proper of you. As a result of your actions this court now has two examples of Sabbath-breaking on the one day: the first a clear case of ignoring the regulations governing the preparation of food for the Sabbath: the second – more serious – involving desecration of the Sabbath by demonic powers. And as if that weren't enough, his pronounced contempt of the Sabbath Laws. I have no more questions of this excellent witness.

JUDGE: Nor has the prisoner I assume?

CLERK: Still no questions, M'Lud!

PROSECUTOR: Call Zachary Ben Simeon of Galilee.

78

CLERK: Call Zachary Ben Simeon of Galilee! (*He is sworn.*)

PROSECUTOR: Now, Zachary Ben Simeon, what is your profession?

WITNESS: A scribe.

PROSECUTOR: Excellent! Then you are used to making accurate records of the spoken word?

WITNESS: My livelihood depends on it, sir.

PROSECUTOR: Can you recall any of the prisoner's speeches, either his political or religious addresses?

WITNESS: Yes, I believe I can.

PROSECUTOR: In your own time –

WITNESS: The one that stands out most clearly was his speech about happiness. He said "Blessed are the poor in spirit for their's is the kingdom of heaven."

PROSECUTOR: More of this poverty nonsense!

WITNESS: No, I don't think he meant it that way. I think he meant the man who isn't obsessed with himself and his own importance finds heaven within him. Then he said: "Blessed are the meek, for they shall inherit the earth."

PROSECUTOR: Forgive me if I laugh. Since when has the land ever been taken by the meek? The strong armies take the land, my friend, not the cowards.

WITNESS: He didn't say cowards. It's only the really strong-in-heart who are gentle and kind, and can afford to wait. One day, he said, they will be the majority on earth.

PROSECUTOR: That will be a long long time a-coming.

WITNESS: I expect it will, but it will come. Next he said: "Blessed are those who mourn, for they shall be comforted."

PROSECUTOR: And pray who will do the comforting?

WITNESS: The moment they realize that life is continuous and that death, like birth, merely another step towards perfection, and realize that all things are but appearances, and the only lasting reality is the Spirit, then there will be no cause to weep when a dear one leaves the body. Rather should we weep if he were left behind and could not join us in the place of reunion.

PROSECUTOR: Any more?

WITNESS: "Blessed are they who hunger and thirst for righteousness, for they shall have their fill. Blessed are the merciful for they shall obtain mercy."

PROSECUTOR: Now, just a minute. You are a good Jew, a strict Jew, are you not?

WITNESS: I try to be.

PROSECUTOR: Then regarding these last two statements, does not a particular body of men – eminent, learned, holy men, spring to your mind?

WITNESS: I hope it refers to many many people, not just one little group.

PROSECUTOR: Would you not feel that description well suited to this holy court?

WITNESS: If it does, then the prisoner has nothing to fear.

PROSECUTOR: Providing he is innocent.

WITNESS: I think he meant much more than that. For I have heard him on several other occasions explaining how divine forgiveness works. He said that we are forgiven as we forgive others – no more and no less. If we forgive fully from our hearts then we too are forgiven all our sins. But if we harbour grievance and revenge, then our own misdeeds turn against us when we come to judgement. In fact we judge ourselves. He said also that whatever we bind to ourselves while on earth we are also bound to in heaven, and what we lose on earth is lost in heaven. All so simple and just! But he went even further, he told a story about a servant who owed his master an enormous sum of money, thousands of pieces of silver and was due for the debtors' prison. And this servant wept and begged the master for time to pay. And the master was so kind, so moved by the man's misery he wrote off the entire debt and told him to forget about repayment. But then the wretched man went after a fellow servant who owned him a few paltry coins and had him up in court for non-payment of debt. Now when the master heard of this he was really angry at such base ingratitude and had him put in jail until he had paid to the very last farthing. "So will my Heavenly Father do to you," said Jesus "if you don't forgive everyone from your deepest heart." (*Pause.*)

PROSECUTOR: Pray continue!

WITNESS: "Blessed are the pure in heart, for they shall see God."

PROSECUTOR: Again the Sanhedrin?

WITNESS: Only they know. It is for each and every reverend lord here to look into his heart and see whether it is pure of all malice, greed, corruption, prejudice, pride and love of power.

PROSECUTOR: My Lord, I think we have heard enough from this witness.

JUDGE: No no, let him continue. This is very interesting.

PROSECUTOR: As your lordship wishes.

WITNESS: "Blessed are the peacemakers for they shall be called the Sons of God. Blessed are they who are persecuted for righteousness sake. Blessed are you when men revile you and persecute you and utter all kinds of evil against you, on my account, rejoice and be glad for your reward is very great in heaven."

JUDGE: I cannot see how this refers to us, Learned Counsel.

WITNESS: And on another occasion he said: "Judge not lest you be judged, for you will be judged just as you judge others, and the measure you give will be the measure you receive." And he said "Don't hit back. If some one hits you, let him hit you again. And if he takes your coat, give him your cloak as well. And if he begs your help, give generously. For that's how you become like God, who is kind and generous to the undeserving."

PROSECUTOR: This is pure anarchy!

WITNESS: I beg to differ. It's sound common sense. Have you ever tried being good to one who hurts you? It's like heaping coals of fire on his head. He cannot bear the shame of it. He is defeated by goodness.

PROSECUTOR: What do you think would happen if everyone were to carry on like this?

WITNESS: There'd be peace on earth and the Spirit of God would dwell among us. It would be unbelievable.

PROSECUTOR: Exactly! It *would* be unbelievable.

JUDGE: Do *you* believe in it?

WITNESS: Yes, I believe it. But I can't see it happening unless you're prepared to give him a chance.

PROSECUTOR: You may stand down.

WITNESS: But I haven't nearly finished.

PROSECUTOR: The court has heard sufficient of this idealistic balderdash to draw its own conclusions.

JUDGE: I would advise this witness to go carefully and to keep his opinions to himself, leaving Holy Church to decide on the meaning of higher moral issues. That will be all!

PROSECUTOR: I don't think I need weary the court with any more of this kind of thing. The last witnesses have provided us with a very clear sample of prisoner's doctrines, doctrines which if they caught on amid the uneducated masses would rapidly cause the wheels of state to grind to a standstill leading to famine, riot, pestilence and starvation. So I should now like to call our key witnesses, witnesses of such learning and erudition, whose testimony in my humble submission will fully and finally substantiate the horrible and insidious charge of blasphemy and apostasy. Crimes against the state are bad enough, but crimes against the Spirit, these are the works of Satan, they rot, they corrupt, they cast into hell fire. Murderers kill the body only. But the blasphemer kills the soul, and all who hear his blasphemy are in danger of eternal damnation.

JUDGE: Quite right.

PROSECUTOR: Call the first of the key witnesses.

CLERK: Call the Very Reverend Eliezer Ben Eliakim, D.D., LL.D., Ph.D. (*He is sworn.*)

PROSECUTOR: Tell the Most Reverend and Learned Judge who you are.

WITNESS: Eliezer Ben Eliakim, a Senior Priest.

PROSECUTOR: And your titles?

WITNESS: Doctor of Law, Doctor of Philosophy, Doctor of Divinity.

PROSECUTOR: Your Reverence, I shall be blunt. Have you ever at any time heard the accused claim divine honours?

WITNESS: I have.

PROSECUTOR: When, Your Reverence?

WITNESS: After an argument with the accused in the Temple Court. He had just made the preposterous statement that if a man were true to his words he would never know death. We replied: "Now we know you're possessed. What about Abraham and the prophets; they're all dead, so who do you think you are?" And he answered: "Honour comes to me from my Father whom you claim as your God, although you can't recognize him. But I know Him. If I said I didn't know Him I'd be like you – a liar. Yes, I have deep knowledge of Him, and am true to His word. And as for Abraham. His heart was proud to see the day of my coming. He saw it and rejoiced to see it." We countered this superb piece of arrogance with the very obvious question: "But you are not yet fifty years old: how then have you seen Abraham?" And he answered . . .

PROSECUTOR: He answered?

82

WITNESS: I can hardly bring myself to repeat it.

JUDGE: Take your time.

WITNESS: He said, "Before Abraham was – I AM." (*Constern-ation*.)

JUDGE: Thank you very much, Your Reverence. It will not be necessary to detain your further.

WITNESS: Thank *you*, Your Grace. I do hope I haven't sinned by repeating that awful blasphemy?

JUDGE: As your spiritual Father-in-God I assure you you have gained richly in grace.

PROSECUTOR: I have two more witnesses, if it please Your Lordship. Call the Chief Scribe to the Temple.

CLERK: Call the Chief Scribe to the Temple. (*He is sworn*.)

JUDGE: My Lord Chief Scribe, I feel the court must humbly beg your pardon for keeping you waiting to give evidence. I had no idea the hearing would take so long.

WITNESS: Think nothing of it, m'dear Caiaphas, think nothing of it. It's been a pleasure I have long looked forward to. Where do you want me to stand? Here? Ah yes. Thank you, dear boy, thank you.

PROSECUTOR: Most Noble Chief Scribe, if it is not putting you to too great inconvenience at this late hour of night, would you kindly tell His Grace here – entirely in your own words – what you can regarding this impious malefactor?

WITNESS: Ah yes, let me see now. Yes. It was about a year ago. He was addressing his so-called disciples – a whole lot of rather elementary stuff – rather first-year theology I thought. Then I heard one of them ask him by what power he achieved his so-called miracles, so I stopped and listened – I could hardly believe my ears. He said something to the effect: It's nothing that I do. It's my heavenly Father in me who does these marvels – My Father and Your Father. But these and greater marvels you shall do. For the Father and I ARE ONE. (*Interruptions*.) Oh yes, indeed he did! Making them all equal, y'see? Himself his friends, all equal with the Most High. Anything else you want to know?

PROSECUTOR: Thank you, I think that is all we need. Thank you again for your great courtesy in coming.

WITNESS: Of course he may have not meant it in quite that sense –

PROSECUTOR: *Thank you*, My Lord Scribe!

WITNESS: – and of course some of the Greek schools contain much the same idea. I studied in Greece, you know. We get books from every religion in the Inner Library, you know. Most interesting, the science of comparative religion, quite fascinating.

PROSECUTOR: Thank you, my lord! Will you *please* stand down?

WITNESS: Oh yes, certainly, delighted to have obliged you. Sorry I can't be of further interest. (*Outburst of discussion.*)

USHER: Silence! Silence in the Court!

JUDGE: Learned Counsel?

PROSECUTOR: M'Lord?

JUDGE: Learned Counsel, have you no wish to question My Lord Chief Scribe further?

PROSECUTOR: No, M'Lord.

JUDGE: Then are you quite satisfied that Sections 69 and 70 of the Act have been fully complied with, sufficiently at any rate, for the Court to reach a verdict to your liking?

PROSECUTOR: M'Lord is most helpful. In the light of his comments I should like to put a further question to Noble Witness. Recall my Lord Chief Scribe.

CLERK: My Lord Chief Scribe, back to the stand please.

WITNESS: What? – No, I must be going. It's late.

PROSECUTOR: M'Lord, please! Just one more question.

WITNESS: You young people never can make up your minds. First you want me, then you don't, then you do. Thought you didn't choose to hear my views?

PROSECUTOR: My Lord Chief Scribe, your views are of paramount interest and their profundity I regret leaves me ignorant and uncomprehending. Fascinating though they be, I regret my question is going to sound very blunt and matter of fact.

WITNESS: Oh all right then, what is it?

PROSECUTOR: Did you, at any time during the discussion you so excellently reported, and so learnedly commented upon, did you at any time hear the prisoner use the secret and forbidden NAME of the Most High?

WITNESS: – Can't say I did.

PROSECUTOR: Are you sure, Noble Scribe?

WITNESS: 'Course I'm sure. But as I've already told you he expressed his One-ness with the Father, and I gave you my considered philosophical annotations thereon. Whether he uses the Secret NAME, or implies it by means of other similarities, it all comes to much the same thing.

PROSECUTOR: No, not exactly.

WITNESS: Is that all you called me back for?

PROSECUTOR: He never in your hearing used the Secret NAME?

WITNESS: How many more times do I have to tell you – may I go now?

PROSECUTOR: Yes, Noble Scribe, you may go now. Call Rabbi Gamaliel.

CLERK: Call Rabbi Gamaliel! (*He is sworn.*)

PROSECUTOR: Rabbi, are you related to the saintly Rabbi Hillel, the preacher of tolerance and moderation, who was so instrumental in preventing bloodshed because of the Census ordered by Augustus Caesar; and who opposed the Zealots, Radicals and trouble makers?

WITNESS: I am his grandson.

PROSECUTOR: You know the prisoner, you have heard him speak?

WITNESS: Indeed I have, many times!

PROSECUTOR: Have you at any time heard the prisoner blaspheme?

WITNESS: No.

PROSECUTOR: Has he not made himself out to be as great as God himself?

WITNESS: You do not understand him. When he has spoken, saying that he was One with the Father, using the most Sacred Name, he did not mean that he, the mere man, the mortal clay, was the Father, but that the Spirit within him – the eternal ever-lasting Christ and the Father – were inseparable from the beginning of the world. Now before you break a blood vessel, I shall quote his exact words which, if you have the least shadow of intuition over and above your dusty law books you will understand his actual as well as his deeper, meaning.

PROSECUTOR: My Lord, I really must protest.

JUDGE: (*to Witness*) Carry on.

WITNESS: He said – listen carefully– "If a man believes in me it is in Him who sent me, not in *me* that he believes. To see me is to see Him who sent me. I have come into this world as a light, so that all those who believe in me may continue no longer in darkness. If a man hears my words and is not true to them, I do not pass sentence on him. I have come to *save* the world, *not* to pass sentence on it. The man who makes me of no account, and does not accept my words has a judge appointed to try him; it is the message I have uttered that will be his judge on the last day. And this, because it is *not on my own authority* that I have spoken, but it was my Father who sent me who commanded me what words I was to say – what message I was to utter. And I know very well that what he commands is eternal life. Everything, then, which I utter, I utter as my Father has bidden me."

JUDGE: Do I then understand you to mean that by this speech the prisoner is retracting the awful blasphemy as testified by the previous witness – that he is contradicting himself?

WITNESS: He's contradicting nothing! It is only a blasphemy to you because you cannot understand him. He never for one moment claimed that he, the carpenter's son, born of woman was co-equal to the Most High. Always has he said: "The Father is greater than I." And again, when his followers called him: "Good Master" he reproved them with these very words: "Why do you call *me* good? There is only one who is good, and that is God." Are these the words of a power-demented lunatic, thinking himself to be God? Or are they words of a truly great man who knows that all goodness is God's, and any goodness we see in man is but a manifestation of that One Goodness? How then do you reconcile this apparent contradiction?

He has said: "He who loses his life shall gain it." And truly this is what he has done. He has lost his little restricting human self in the Infinite Self of the Father. The potsherd is broken and the water released to the Fountainhead. He thinks nothing of himself as the potsherd. But if you begin to understand him you see not the potsherd, but the limitless ocean of bliss we call God. It was the Voice of that boundless Ocean that uttered: "The Father and I are One." And it is the thunder of that Ocean throughout the seven eternities that proclaims: "I Am That I Am." But you heard only the voice of a man born of woman so you cried: "Stone him! blasphemy! blasphemy!" (*Interruptions.*) He has transcended the limitations of the flesh and become One-with-Him. The little becomes the Great. The Great does not become the little. It cannot! Do you understand me?

PROSECUTOR: No!!

JUDGE: You are an Essene, I think you said?

WITNESS: I am.

JUDGE: Then I suggest you get back to Qumran before I have you on similar charges.

WITNESS: I only came forth from my monastery because I thought (vainly it seems) that what little understanding I may have of him, I may be able to share with you and thus prevent a blasphemy that will echo down the ages even unto the end of time.

JUDGE: And what exactly do you mean by that?

WITNESS: You know full well what I mean! (*Uproar.*)

PROSECUTOR: M'Lord, will you please hold this witness in contempt?

JUDGE: Guards! Have this witness escorted to the city gates, and arrest him if he tries to re-enter before the Passover is concluded – I trust, Learned Counsel, your next witness will do better than this?

PROSECUTOR: I have no more witnesses, M'Lord.

JUDGE: No more witnesses? Then, Learned Counsel, before you rest your case I should again remind you of the relevant sections of the Act.

PROSECUTOR: As your Lordship pleases.

JUDGE: Section 64, as you know, establishes the Grand Sanhedrin as the highest authority for all serious cases and questions of law. Section 65 establishes the Grand Sanhedrin as the sole legal authority empowered to pass sentence of death in all cases of apostasy. However, this section was recently revoked by our Roman overlords, so that the court is now required to refer all persons so convicted to the Governor General's Supreme Court for ratification – usually a mere formality. Section 66, as you know, requires that all such cases shall be heard before a Plenum of all Two and Seventy Members of this Grand Sanhedrin. All of which I am repeating, at this later stage so that the record may be in perfect order when set before the Governor General. So far, so good. But now I must once more draw your attention, and that of all present, to Sections 69 and 70.

PROSECUTOR: M'Lord, I think we can now safely assume –

JUDGE: We can assume *nothing*, Learned Counsel. We are in a court of law, and the law is concerned only with the facts of law, and the facts are stated thus: I shall read them to you. "Section 69: The

87

evidence of at least two witnesses is required for corroboration in every such case of apostasy." "Section 70: The incriminating evidence of the said witnesses must coincide in minute and incidental details." Now you have called a number of witnesses, but it will fall upon you to satisfy all two and seventy members of this holy court that such evidence, of two or more witnesses; coincidental in minute and incidental details has so been irrefutably presented. And while you may very well be in a position to secure a conviction on certain lesser counts not requiring such stringent rules of evidence, it may still not be possible, as matters stand, to so do on the more serious charges for which the punishment is death.

PROSECUTOR: M'Lord, I know. But I think –

JUDGE: So with your permission, Learned Counsel, I shall now address the prisoner.

PROSECUTOR: By every possible means.

JUDGE: The prisoner as you will all have observed has entered no pleas in his own defence. He has refused all legal representation, he has declined to cross-examine his accusers. He has, by his very demeanour, made an extremely unfavourable impression upon me. I am not even sure if he is willing to recognize the jurisdiction of this court. In fact I hardly see he should, having flouted the authority of God and his holy prophets, so what is a mere court like this to a man who has claimed the kingdom of heaven as his rightful demesne? But despite the most disrespectful and unwise manner in which he has conducted himself during this hearing, it is my duty as his Judge to give him every last opportunity to redeem himself, and speak up to save himself, before it is too late. I shall now make one final appeal for him to testify, before I am compelled to sum up and have your lordships consider your verdict. Jesus, son of Joseph. You have now heard the evidence. Have you no answer to the charges and accusations these men bring against you?

CLERK: You will answer His Lordship!

JUDGE: (sighs) Very well – perhaps instead you will tell us something about yourself – about your friends, your party members? What kind of people are they? What are you all trying to achieve? What do you think you have to teach us, the divinely appointed spiritual authorities, that hasn't adequately and fully been covered, once and for all time, in the Torah, the sacred books of the Prophets and of the Law? Why do you not submit yourself to the Authority

88

of Holy Mother Church which errs not in its teaching, because it is divinely appointed by God who can neither deceive nor be deceived?

JESUS: I have spoken openly before the whole world. My teaching has been given in the synagogue and in the Temple where all the Jews foregather. Nothing that I have said was said in secret. Why do you question me? Ask those who listened to me what my words were. They know well enough what I said. (*One of the dock guards strikes him across the face.*)

GUARD: You insolent fellow! Is that how you answer His Lordship, the High Priest?

JESUS: If there was any harm in what I said, tell us what was harmful in it. If not, why do you strike me?

JUDGE: Prisoner, we have all heard your teachings, and understood their import. The point is – *do you*? I am therefore going to put a question to you – just one single question and I want you to answer it. You may consider carefully before replying. But answer it you must, and answer it you will. *Jesus, son of Joseph, are you the Christ?*

JESUS: What if I tell you? You will never believe me. And if I ask you questions, I know you will not answer them, nor acquit me.

JUDGE: (*rising to his feet*) Jesus of Nazareth, I adjure you by the Living God, are you the Christ, the Son of God?

JESUS: Your own lips have said it. I AM! (*Consternation.*)
And moreover I tell you this – you will see the Son of Man sitting at the right hand of God's Power and coming in glory on the clouds of heaven! (*Uproar.*)

CLERK: Silence! Order in Court. Silence! Silence!

JUDGE: You heard it! You all heard it! I tear my garments! Oh blasphemy, blasphemy. Note it well, all of you. You all heard his blasphemy for yourselves! What need have we for further witnesses? (*Uproar.*)

CLERK: Silence! Silence!

PROSECUTOR: Our corroborating second witness, in every detail! Thank you, M'Lord.

JUDGE: Reverend my Lords, Elders of this holy court. You may now retire and consider your verdict.

CHIEF ELDER: There is no need for us to retire. The man is self-confessed and self-condemned.

JUDGE: Then what is your verdict?

CHIEF ELDER: Guilty on all counts!

JUDGE: And what is your sentence?

CHIEF ELDER: Death!

JUDGE: And so say all of you?

CHIEF ELDER: We do.

JUDGE: So be it. It is the will of this holy court that our verdict and our sentence be ratified, upheld and sustained by the Governor General in the Imperial Supreme Court in accordance with the Laws of Rome, and that all evidence and matters having to do with these hearings shall be immediately placed before the said Supreme Court and there so be ratified upheld and sustained.

Jesus Ben Joseph. It is the sentence of this holy court that you be taken hence to appear before the Governor General and the Supreme Court, and thereafter to the place so appointed where you be hung by the hands until dead, and that you do be buried without honour amid common felons in accordance with the law so enacted. Take away the prisoner.

CLERK: Take away the prisoner and do unto him as you have been commanded. Be upstanding in Court for His Grace, the Most Reverend Joseph Caiaphas, Doctor of Divinity, High Priest of Jerusalem, Primate of All Israel, Lord Chief Justice of the Courts Ecclesiastical, and Lord President of the Grand Council of the Sanhedrin. (*Judge leaves court.*)

CLERK: Hear ye, hear ye, hear ye! Your duties being discharged honourably and faithfully, to the upholdment of our laws and the satisfaction of our Most Noble King, his crown and dignity, go ye all hence your several ways in righteousness, in peace and in God's good keeping. Hail Caesar!

END OF COURT TRANSCRIPT.

Officially Approved

NZ

Amended

JM

Adjudged Correct in all matter and substance

JB

Note: *Copy to H.E. The Governor General.*   **Immediate!**

TO HIS GRACE
THE PRIMATE

a.d. IV. Nōn Apr.
Anno Urbis Conditae
*DCCLXXXVI**

Your Grace,

Your Memorandum marked: **"MOST URGENT"** and your numerous enclosures have been received and noted.

They shall be placed before HIS EXCELLENCY when he emerges from his bath.

C. S. SCIPIO
A.D.C. to HIS EXCELLENCY THE GOVERNOR GENERAL

POST SCRIPTUM

Would you kindly use Roman dating in future?

It would greatly oblige the ADMINISTRATION and expedite your suite.

* Note: April 2, A.D. 33.

THE RESIDENCY, IERVSALEM

A.U.C. DCCLXXXVI
a.d. IV Nōn Apr.

Your Grace,

Do you really expect me to be able to read all this and to arrive at a reasoned judgement in the short time remaining before the Courts close for the Passover?

I have a number of important matters scheduled for my attention this morning, so this case must be processed through the usual channels before I can give it proper attention.

I shall do my best to allocate it Priority Rating when the Holy Days are over.

Hail Caesar!

PONTIVS PILATVS
GOVERNOR GENERAL

ENCLOSURES: III
I Copy Official Court Transcript (Ecclesiastic)
I Copy Intelligence Report No. V/I.C. (*SECRET*)
I Copy Background Report No. II/I.C. (*CONFIDENTIAL*)

OFFICE OF THE
HIGH PRIEST

MOST IMMEDIATE AND URGENT

Ante Diem Quartum, Nonias Apriles
Anno Urbis Conditae DCCLXXX VI

Re. Jesus of Nazareth

Your Excellency,

I really must *insist* that you give this case your prompt and immediate attention. I cannot emphasize sufficiently that every moment's delay in carrying out sentence is fraught with danger. The condemned is by his own admission guilty on each and every count requiring the Supreme Penalty. As I said in my previous communication, we have a law, and by that law he must die.

I have done all I can – sitting up most of the night doing my duty by Caesar and by Almighty God. Now it is up to you!

The condemned *must*, repeat, *must*, be executed before the Passover as precept and example. This is vital to present Security. I am therefore taking the liberty of returning to you the Court Transcript etc. herewith, that you may so ratify, sustain and uphold Our Verdict and Our Sentence.

Hail Caesar, etc.

CAIAPHAS JERUSALEM

ENCL.: III
I Copy Court Transcript (returned)
I Copy Intelligence Report No. V/I.C. (**SECRET**)
I Copy Background Report No. II/I.C. (**CONFIDENTIAL**)

POLICE DEPARTMENT

SPECIAL BRANCH

[Temple Precinct]

Subject	Routine Interrogation of Political Prisoner
Name of Prisoner	Jesus, son of Joseph (self-styled prophet and one-time joiner's assistant)
Present	One Capt. Two Lieuts. Two Sgts. Five Plain-clothes-men.
Date	Nisan 14, 3794 (a.d. IV Kal A.U.C. DCCLXXXVI)

REPORT OF INTERROGATION

Prisoner was brought down shortly after midnight of today's date imediately consequant to Committal Proceedings in the Ecclesiastic Court (His Grace J. CAIAPHAS Presiding) and was questioned at length but with results being negative.

Severel of the above officers taking part having attended Court were aggreeved at the contemptuous demeaner in which prisoner had deported himself during said proseedings. So they roughed him up a bit, but he remained silent provoking the lawful officers thereby.

It was decided to test out his alledged powers of (a) fortune-telling (b) clarevoyence and (c) professying as per the following methods

VIZ: Prisoner was blindfolded, then each offiser present took turns to strike him on the face and upon sundry bodily parts demanding that he demonstrate his said alledged powers by assertaining the name/names of the striker/strikers. He failed miseribly. From which opperations we evinsed that his alledged powers are nil.

Later, some of the Mess Orderlies came down to join in the fun. They to endevored to provoke prisoner to demonstrate his alledged powers by professying as to whom would strike him next. We promised him that if he got just one answer right we'd lay off him.

But he did not.

It is thus hereby the considered opinion of the Special Branch that said prisoner is a complete fraud.

Copies To: (I) H.E. The Governor General (II) H.G. The Primate. (III) Clerk of the Supreme Court. (IV) Mgr. Jacob Ben Jacob (Recorder of Prophesies)

GOVERNOR GENERAL'S MEMORANDVM

To THE LORD PRESIDENT
OF THE COUNCIL
OF THE GRAND SANHEDRIN

Date. *Idem.*

(I) HIS EXCELLENCY has received the LORD PRESIDENT'S "Most Urgent and Immediate" Memo and appended documents.

(II) HIS EXCELLENCY has perused said documents.

(III) HIS EXCELLENCY has taken note of your verdict and your sentence.

(IV) However, before ratifying same, HIS EXCELLENCY proposes to examine the Prisoner.

(V) But, as the Eve of the native Feast of the Passover is now upon us, and as all good Jews who might venture into the "pagan" Precincts of Noble CAESAR'S MOST AUGUST SUPREME COURT at this time would thereby become "defiled", the Matter should, in the normal course of events, be held over until the conclusion of the religious festivities.

(VI) HIS EXCELLENCY however has kindly and graciously consented to resolve your dilemma by conducting an open air Hearing from the Rostrum of the Antonia Palace (Residency).

Trusting that this will meet with your requirements.

C. S. SCIPIO

A.D.C. to HIS EXCELLENCY THE GOVERNOR GENERAL

TREASURY

TEMPLE OF THE MOST HIGH GOD OF ISRAEL

Received the sum of £30=0=0 (say, *Thirty pieces of Silver*)

For information received leading to the arrest and detention of one, Jesus, Son of Joseph, of the Town and Urban District of Nazareth, self-styled prophet and one-time joiner's assistant.

Date   Nisan 10. 3794

SIGNED *JUDAS ISCARIOT*

For Official Use Only . . . . Official Endorsement.

The above sum was later returned to the Treasury by the above J. Iscariot, claiming false representation of the facts. The Treasury refused acceptance as there is no machinery for dealing with such eventualities. Whereupon, said J. Iscariot used abusive language, flinging said sum on the floor of this office. Said J. Iscariot reproached all and sundry, shouting "I have sinned. I have betrayed the blood of an innocent man!" The Chief Accountant was called who informed said J. Iscariot that this was no concern of the Treasury. Whereupon said J. Iscariot ran out and committed 'felo de se" (copy to Coroner's Office).

It has now been ruled by Mgr Barnabas, Head of Treasury, that these monies may not be re-credited to Treasury A/C, as they are alleged to be the price of blood (Viz. Subsec 4/b, paras 5, 9 Tres. Regs. Herod 1) but should be utilized for the purchase of the disused potter's field as a burial ground for strangers, thereby relieving City Rates. Said burial ground, when consecrated to be named: "Haceldama".

A.C.M.

ASSISTANT ACCOUNTANT

GOVERNOR GENERAL'S MEMORANDVM

From: A.D.C.

To: H.E. The G.G.

Excellency,

> *The H.P.J. (P.A.-I.) is here and insists on an Audience.*
> *Shall I send him away?*

NO, I'D BETTER SEE HIM. BUT INTERRUPT IF HE STAYS TOO LONG.
>   *P.P.*

S. P. Q. R.

THE RESIDENCY, IERVSALEM

Date. *Idem*

Your Grace,

At your request I have personally examined the Prisoner in Open Court and in Chambers. I find his silence in public irritating and not a little surprising. But when speaking to me privately in Chambers I find his answers intriguing and his arguments almost irrefutable.

As far as I can see, the Temple has a very weak case. Under your own Law, Secs 69/70 there appears to be insufficient agreement required from at least two or more witnesses to secure conviction. As for the Civil Charges, I cannot find in these sufficient grounds to warrant his execution. The SUPREME COURT is sorely over-worked at this time. Civil Rightists, Sit-Downs, Anarchists, and self-appointed (your pardon!) "Messiahs" are overloading the Imperial Judiciary and impeding the smooth normal flow and dispensation of Justice.

Would you therefore be satisfied if we settled for a count of "Unlawful Assembly" and convicted accordingly? Alternatively, under "The Emergency Powers Act" (still in force after fifty years) I could detain him indefinitely, or, at least until the present atmosphere of rebellion and general unrest has somewhat abated.

To my mind that might be the simplest, swiftest and most just solution.

Hail Caesar!

PONTIVS PILATVS
GOVERNOR GENERAL

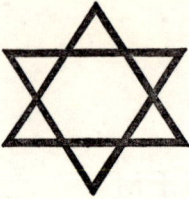

PALACE OF
THE PRIMATE

Date. *Idem*

Your Excellency,

This simply will not do!

Imprison him, and his followers will demonstrate and riot until we release him. Far be it for a mere Jew to question the actions of a Noble Roman, but have you even read those sections of the Court Transcript I marked for your particular attention?

We have a Law, and under that Law (i.e. Secs 1, 6, 13, 16, 18, and 30) he must die, on each and every count. There is no possible alternative and you must uphold, sustain and carry out our Sentence without further delay.

For your immediate guidance I enclose an extract of the above relevant sections.

Hail Caesar!

CAIAPHAS JERUSALEM

PRIMATE OF ALL ISRAEL

ENCLOSURES

FOR THE GUIDANCE AND ASSISTANCE OF HIS EXCELLENCY THE GOVERNOR GENERAL OF THE PROVINCE OF JUDÆA.

Extracts from "An Act for the Suppression and Punishment of Blasphemy, Heresy, Apostasy, False-prophecy, Wonder working by-the-power-of-Beelzebub, Incitement to Rebellion, and Defiance of the Authority and Rulings of the Grand Sanhedrin."

SECTION	PENALTY
1 "Whosoever knowingly and willingly shall break the law of the Sabbath or any other Commandment of the Torah has despised the Word of the Lord."	On first offence he shall be warned. If he refuses to heed the warning and repeats the offence, he shall be punished by death.
6 "The Grand Sanhedrin in the Temple of Jerusalem hands down the law in the Name of God. God himself respects these decisions."	Defiance of the Authority of the Grand Sanhedrin shall be punished by death. Defiance of the decisions of the Grand Sanhedrin shall be punished by death.
13 "Whosoever defies or ridicules the officiating priests in Jerusalem shall die."	
16 "Whosoever takes the name of the Lord in vain is a blasphemer."	The convicted blasphemer shall die. His body shall be hung from a cross.
18 "Whosoever arrogates to himself divine honours or rights is a blasphemer."	Before the end of the day of execution the body of the blasphemer will be taken from the cross and buried without honour.
30 "An enticer to apostasy is a Jew who persuades another Jew to abandon his faith."	In dealing with an enticer, consideration of kinship or humanity should play no part. If proven guilty, the enticer will be stoned to death.

GOVERNOR GENERAL'S MEMORANDVM

Your Grace,

Thank you for drawing my attention to the relevant Sections of your Act.

This has confirmed my opinion that the matter is entirely Ecclesiastical, and does not come within the purview nor jurisdiction of The Imperial Supreme Court.

You must deal with the matter yourselves.

Hail Caesar!

S.C.S

Per pro PONTIVS PILATVS

ECCLESIASTICAL COURT OF THE GRAND SANHEDRIN

JUDGE'S MEMORANDUM

To H.E. the G.G.
From Lord President of the Courts Ecclesiastical

Re. Jesus of Nazareth

His Excellency the Governor General must surely be aware that under the recent modifications to the "Rome–Israel Treaty" the Ecclesiastic Courts no longer have power to carry out the Death Sentence and are obliged to refer all such convictions to the Imperial Supreme Court for their ratification and execution, which shall not be reasonably denied.

Z.N.
Per pro The Lord President

C.P.P.

Friday

My Darling Husband,

You know I'm not hysterical nor given to fanciful imagination, but *please* listen to me. I wanted to see you all day but you've been so busy I couldn't get word to you. And you had left for Court when I arose this morning, after a hellish night.

Do you remember that time on the long trip out from Rome when I dreamed our carriage overturned and we were all killed? Remember how I made you examine the axle and we found the wheel was just about to come off: and how if we'd continued it might have come off on that twisty dangerous mountain road? Well, I was right wasn't I?

Last night I had the most ghastly dream. But like the chariot dream it was more than a dream. It was intensely vivid and has left me very shaken. I saw this prisoner, Jesus the Nazarene, mobbed by angry screaming people trying to kill him. Then suddenly he was surrounded by light, the most beautiful golden light unlike anything I've ever seen when awake. He seemed to be lifted up and brought towards me. I looked right into his eyes. I can't tell you how it has affected me! They were the most wonderful terrible eyes. It was like looking into the face of a god . . .

Dear Husband, please please be careful!! This is no ordinary man. He may well be an emissary of Great Jupiter (they say His messengers travel in humble guises) and to harm one of the Them would surely be a crime against Heaven and would bring ruin and retribution on all of us.

I'm not being superstitious. Indeed, you have so often praised me for my sound common sense. So when I speak to you like this I beg you not to regard me lightly.

I shall speak to you – I hope – after supper.

Your loving
CLAUDIA

104

P.P.

Dearest One,

Please don't distress yourself unduly! I have just examined this Jesus fellow in Chambers, and you are quite right – he is no ordinary zealot, hooligan, civil-rightist, anarchist, nor (as they would have me believe) extreme nationalist. He appears to be a pacifist and something of an idealistic dreamer; so much so, I can scarcely follow his more lyrical flights of fancy.

The charges against him seem to me rather spurious, and all based on tiresome technicalities of their bewildering religion. Indeed, the very size of the Court Transcript – a legal mountain to crush a religious molehill – was sufficient to make me suspect the true motives of "His Grace" Caiaphas and all his holy cant.

How I loathe their endless tiresome boring Oriental intrigues, their complicated plots, their tangled arguments which, to our western minds, seem such a complete and utter waste of time! I think it is high time we looked for someone less obnoxious than "Reverend C" to fill the See of Solomon.

But, darling, I think I may have a solution that will outwit them at their own little game. Tomorrow, when the Passover begins (I *had* been hoping you and I might have had a little holiday during this feast! But we haven't a hope in Hades) it is the custom that I release to them a prisoner under sentence of death. So I shall offer them the choice of Jesus or Barabbas – if only to watch "Rev. C" s face when I do it. Barabbas, incidentally is that vicious anarchist leader who nearly plunged the whole Province into full-scale civil war and, had he succeeded, would have cost "Rev. C" his Archiepiscopal throne. Rome has made it abundantly clear that any such repetition will lead to very heavy reprisals, and the old humbug was shaking with relief when we caught Barabbas, the ringleader.

As for Jesus, his dignified silence doesn't help when I'm trying my damnedest to get him acquitted. I suppose I shall have to take note at least of some of the civil charges, or I shall never hear the end of it. Frankly, he *has* been a bit of a nuisance and has wasted a lot of my time, so I may have to convict on a minor count.

Dearest Claudia, I don't think you silly, nor superstitious. In fact I love you for your tender compassion and for going on loving me when I am obliged to perform so many unpleasant, not to say, rather brutal, duties to keep some sort of law and order in this desperate backwood of a Province.

No, I won't let them get away with too much.

Promise!
In haste
PONTIVS

GOVERNOR GENERAL'S MEMORANDVM

TO THE PRIMATE

Very well, then. I shall re-examine him and let you know my findings as soon as possible. I cannot promise that I shall alter my previous opinion.

PONTIVS PILATVS

Forma XB/II/c

DAILY ROVTINE ORDERS

Unit: CITY GARRISON (IERVSALEM) Xth LEGION
Date: a.d. V Id. Feb. DCCLXXXVI

Testudo Socket-pins and Section-bolts, used for gaming purposes, undesirability of

(I) The Officer Commanding has noted with extreme displeasure the growing practice of misusing Testudo Socket-Pins and Section-Bolts for gaming purposes causing serious losses and wastage, with very serious detriment to the efficiency of said Testudo. This will cease forthwith.

(II) All Ranks are strenuously reminded that the efficiency and safety of the Testudo in siege operations and especially in Riot Control lies in the firm and speedy interlocking of shields to provide an instant, impenetrable but highly mobile armour for troops. The loss or absence of a single Socket-Pin or Section-Bolt can seriously weaken the entire structure of the Testudo, exposing the troops sheltering therein to grievous and unnecessary dangers; particularly in cases when street-width Testudos are formed for the immediate and effective street clearance of rioters.

(III) Each soldier is responsible for the care and maintenance of his issue-set of Socket-Pins and Section-Bolts and will be severely punished if any are found missing during Cohort Commanders' Inspections.

(IV) CROSSES, CRUCIFIXION
With effect from today's date Crosses, Crucifixion (Type E) will be drawn as required from ARMOURY and not as heretofore from CARPENTER'S STORES.

(V) Nails, ditto, however will continue to be drawn from Regimental Blacksmith. They will be returned after use and memento hunting will cease forthwith unless in the opinion of the Officer i/c Execution nails have been bent or damaged.

(VI)   TIMBER SHORTAGE

Owing to current timber shortage in the Province, Crosses, Crucifixion (all types) will be thoroughly cleansed and returned to Stores after usage (see STANDING ORDER XV/S/I).

(VII)   There has been noticeable slackness in respect of (V) and (VI) above. This slackness will cease w.e.f. today's date.

(IX)   The Garrison Concert scheduled for Tuesday is cancelled and will take place instead on Thursday at the same hour. Troops off duty on Tuesday may, if they wish, continue to avail themselves of the Herodian Hippodrome for recreational purposes.

(X)   PUNISHMENT SQUAD

Soldiers detailed to Punishment Squad are entitled to one extra day's leave per month as per the following:

(A) After carrying out three scourgings with the Flagrum or Six Scourgings with the Flagellum.

(B) After carrying out two crucifixions.

VOLUNTEERS for above duties are entitled to one half-day's extra leave per each of (A) but not totalling an aggregate of more than two and one half days' extra leave in any one month.

(XI)   BRASSES, POLISHING OF

There has been noticeable slackness in the polishing of Helmets, Brass, Other Ranks, since the last Inspection by G.O.C. Xth. To obviate this tendency there will be snap inspections by Unit Commanders without prior notice, and offenders punished with heavy fatigues.

(XII)   G. and H. Cohorts will draw Tropical Kit tomorrow at 08.30 hrs prior to their departure for Border Duties on the Egyptian Frontier. They will report to S.M.O. at 09.45 hrs for Medical Inspection and preventative medicinal treatment against Sandfly Fever.

N.A.M.

ADJVTANT

S. P. Q. R.

TO HIS MAIESTY
HEROD ANTIPAS REX
Hasmonaean Palace
Iervsalem I

Sire,

In the course of examining a prisoner, one Jesus of Nazareth, the alleged prophet and wonder-worker, it transpired that he hails from Galilee, thus coming under the jurisdiction of Your Majesty, the Tetrarch.

I am furthermore informed that this prisoner is the self same Galilean wonder-worker often spoken of by Your Majesty and concerning whom you have expressed the desire (correct me if I am wrong) to see him in the flesh.

In addition, I am led to believe there exists a general conviction in certain quarters that this prisoner is either a re-incarnation of Elija, or Elias (forgive me, but I always get these two confused) or else a resurrected version of John the Baptiser whom you had reason to have beheaded!!

If he should happen to be the latter, doubtless you would be the first to recognize him?

Knowing of these your several interests I am herewith adjourning my court and remitting the prisoner immediately to the Hasmonaean Palace along with (for your information and convenience) the court transcript which contains a formidable report of his many alleged miracles and wonders.

Regarding these I wish Your Majesty every possible success. For I have questioned him exhaustively, both in court and privately in chambers, failing utterly to draw him into any least demonstration of his reputed extra-terrestrial powers. Personally, I rather like the fellow, and find his obvious sincerity impressive.

109

His answers are few, but intriguing. He seems completely oblivious to the very mortal danger in which he now stands. So I am sincerely hoping that, as he claims to be a "king", he will be more forthcoming and obliging when confronted face to face by a *real king* as opposed to a mere Governor General.

I ask merely that should you be successful in provoking him into any worth-while demonstration, you would kindly let me know immediately as this would prove an important factor in weighing the case on its merits.

But, as I have already made bold to point out, the prisoner is Galilean and has little business in my court; more properly coming within your more able jurisdiction. Furthermore, as the case is largely based upon abstruse points of theology and Jewish religious law I am confident that, with your greater learnedness of such matters, you would be far better fitted to deal with him, and should graciously take the whole matter into your more competent hands.

In anticipation of this I am submitting to you the full indictment, also my personal copy of the court transcript.

Hail Caesar!

PONTIVS PILATVS,

BY IMPERIAL WARRANT

GOVERNOR GENERAL OF

PROVINCE OF IVDAEA

ENCLOSURES:
Indictment
Court Transcript

 **HR**III

a.d. IV Nōn apr.
A.V.C. DCCLXXXVI

MOST NOBLE GOVERNOR GENERAL,

How very considerate of you!

We have indeed heard much of this Jesus from our Head Steward, Chusa, whose wife, Joanna, I have learned could be numbered among his most ardent admirers, and who assures me that his many alleged wonders are by no means fictitious. So pray send him over immediately as We have long desired to see him for Ourself and discover his true identity.

We sincerely trust he is not John the Baptiser, as when last We parted company the circumstances were a little unfortunate!

We are grateful indeed that you should have thought of Us (naturally with no ulterior motive) so We shall send you prompt word should anything interesting transpire. You flatter me by thinking I should succeed in provoking a miracle, when Our August Procurator has apparently failed. But even should a minor one take place – such as curing Our arthritis – We would be less than gracious if We did not grant him royal pardon.

Hail Caesar!

HEROD ANTIPAS REX

H R III

Nisan 14 Anno Mundi 3744

MOST NOBLE GOVERNOR GENERAL,

We are most grievously disappointed!! What could have proved a diverting morning turned out a complete fiasco. This Galilean is most certainly not Elijah nor Elisha, nor (Thank God) John the Baptiser, but a tongue-tied artisan with even less powers than a bazaar-stall conjurer. We did our utmost to induce him into working a miracle – a small one – any little sign of prophetic or supranormal abilities. Had he but relieved Our arthritis We should have freed him, graciously and immediately. But alas, no. He merely stood there listening to the recital of charges in a detached silence.

We even treated him with full "kingly honours", seated him upon Our throne, clothed him in royal purple, put a "sceptre" in his hand, while Our humorous guards set upon his head a "crown" of their own design which should, to say the least, have *pricked* him into conceding us the courtesy of some small sign or wonder.

But, alas, nothing! Merely a tedious silence. All very wearying and tiresome!

We must confess We are somewhat displeased that the Procurator should deem it necessary to burden the Tetrarch with matters more properly the concern of the Roman Supreme Court, when Our sole purpose in seeing the prisoner was not to judge him but to determine whether or not he happened to be a re-animated John the Baptiser. And now that Our mind has been set at ease We are returning him to you, forthwith, albeit slightly the worse for wear as Our guards do not take kindly to dull or obdurate prisoners.

We do not say he is guilty. We do not say he is innocent. You must deal with him as you see fit.

Hail Caesar!

p.p HEROD ANTIPAS REX

DICTATED, BUT NOT SIGNED BY "HEROD ANTIPAS REX"

ENCLOSURES: 1 Court Transcript and divers documents.

112

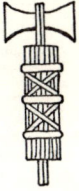

a.d. IV Nōn Apr.
A.U.C. DCCLXXXVI

TO HIS MAIESTY THE TETRARCH,
HEROD ANTIPAS REX,
Hasmonaean Palace,
Iervsalem I

The Governor General regrets that he should have wasted His Majesty, The Tetrarch's most valuable time, but is grateful that he should have examined the prisoner and endeavoured to prove or disprove his alleged powers.

The Governor General will therefore convict him on a lesser count and sentence accordingly.

Hail Caesar!

S.C.S.

DICTATED, BUT NOT SIGNED BY

PONTIVS PILATVS

BY IMPERIAL WARRANT

GOVERNOR GENERAL OF THE

PROVINCE OF IVDAEA

THE RESIDENCY, IERVSALEM

HIS GRACE
THE PRIMATE,

Date: *Idem*

Re. Jesus of Nazareth

Your Grace,

Neither H.M. King Herod III, to whom was referred the above case, nor the Imperial Court could find sufficient grounds to uphold a conviction requiring the Supreme Penalty.

The Imperial Court is hereby acquitting him on all such charges.

However, although I am still not entirely satisfied (from the evidence laid before me) that he should not be released immediately, I am willing to convict on a lesser (civil) count (Number IX in your original memo: "Divers offences liable to cause a breach of Caesar's Peace").

I hereby sentence him to a Scourging, to be carried out immediately; after which he is to go free. Trusting this information will be satisfactory to your good self, to the Grand Sanhedrin and to the Elders and Rulers of the Temple.

Hail Caesar!

PONTIVS PILATVS

ORDERLY ROOM

Unit: D. COHORT Xth LEGION   *a.d. III Nōn. Apr.*

DAILY RETVRNS (PVNISHMENTS AND FATIGVES)

Forma IX/B/c

Offenders	No.	Offence	Punishment	Carried Out
Defaulters	V	late on parade	X lashes	*P.V.* (Sgt)
Defaulters	III	dirty brasses	V extra drills	*A.S.* (Sgt)
Defaulters	I	insufficient attention at arms drill	XIV Days C.B. with Drill	*S.C.* (Cpl)
Defaulter	I	Facial Insubordination	XV lashes	*P.V.* (Sgt)
Defaulters	II	A.W.O.L.	Referred to O.C. Xth Leg.	*A.S.* (Sgt)
Political Prisoner (Civilian)		Sundry offences contrary to the Emergency Powers Act	Scourged Flagrum Mk IIb LX Lashes	*S.C.* (Cpl)

Copies to (I) Adjutant D and B Cohorts
(II) R.S.M. Discips.
(III) Clerk i/c Files

Note. This Forma supersedes Forma IX/B/a

Unit: Xth LEGION (CITY GARRISON IERVSALEM)
R.S.O. No: LXXIX/B
Subject: *"FLAGRVM" OPERATION OF:*
Date: a.d. XV Kal. Oct. DCCLXXXIII

The Correct Procedures for operating Flagra Mk IIa and Mk IIb (Modified) are as follows:—

   (I)   Prisoner will be securely bound in accordance with Procedure as detailed in S.O. CLIVa, and bindings will be inspected and approved by N.C.O. i/c Scourging.

  (II)   N.C.O. will inspect Flagrum selected and test for faults. Flagra Mk IIa are armed with animal knuckle bones, and Flagra Mk IIb (Modified) are additionally armed with lead twin-balls; both to cause optimum cutaneous detriment. These have a tendency to work loose and should be inspected before and after use.

 (III)   N.C.O. will call Operators to Attention.

 (IV)   On being called to Attention, both left and right-hand operator will raise his Flagrum, bringing the arm backwards into striking position; handle held outwards at XLV degrees, thongs hanging clear of the body of the Operator.

  (V)   On the count of "I", right-hand operator will bring arm smartly forward causing end of thongs to strike prisoner.

 (VI)   On the count of "II", left-hand operator will do likewise from his position at opposite side of Prisoner.

(VII)   Right-hand operator will continue to strike on "Odd Numbers" until called to a halt. Left-hand operator will continue to strike on "Even Numbers" until likewise called to a halt. He will cause his blows to fall neatly crosswise on the marks caused by right-hand operator.

 (IX)   Blows will commence slightly below the neck and will work downwards evenly until reaching the feet. Unless instructed to the contrary, both operators will then continue to work upwards again to the neck.

  (X)   Blows will be evenly timed and evenly spaced. They will be given with severe but evenly graded striking force in order to ensure maximum and universal discomfiture.

(XI)   Unless otherwise instructed, care should be taken when striking neck and shoulder area to avoid detriment to countenance.

(XII)   Having worked from neck to feet and from feet back to neck, prisoner will be unbound, reversed, and re-bound to face operators who will continue as before; avoiding heart and genital areas unless otherwise instructed.

(XIII)   Operators will be changed after delivering fifty blows each if N.C.O. i/c perceives a falling off in striking power owing to fatigue factor.

(XIV)   Under no circumstances will operators talk to or address prisoner during any of the above.

For variations, amendments and addenda to above see Supplemental Orders X/B/VI/c and X/B/VI/e.
Supplemental Orders LX/d/a to LX/d/f are cancelled.

J.A.M.

Adjvtant

COUNCIL OF THE GRAND SANHEDRIN

ANNAS BEN SETH. D.D.

My Dear Governor General,

Pray forgive an interfering old man having his say, but it is sometimes the privilege of old age to be tiresome; and the right (nay, the duty) of one who once held Highest Office to speak his mind and offer what little assistance and advice he is able, lest another harrowing mistake be made, and many innocent men and women have to suffer.

May I be frank? May I, without wishing to cause any offence to your High Position and Noble Person give you a little word of advice?

You have held office only these last six summers. I have lived here all my life, as has my Son-in-law, Joseph Caiaphas, who has (since my retirement) been our High Priest full fifteen years. So, between us, we know and understand our people rather too well! I am a Jew. You are a Roman (a very Noble Roman) I am not presuming to criticize – Heaven forbid !– I am merely stating that Rome is not Judaea and the Roman mind, so excellent in all things, is not the Jewish mind, which, perforce, makes it exceeding hard for any Procurator who has been with us so short a time to judge us, or our motives, correctly.

Thus, when we welcomed you here with joy and fullest honours it soon became evident (forgive me being blunt!) that, through no fault of your own, the Colonial Office had – let us say – not been very thorough in their briefing; having failed to help you fully comprehend us Jews and what our Religion means to us. You can tax us, imprison us, kill us; but one thing you cannot do is to offend the least jot or tittle of our Religious Principles.

This the Senate understands.

This, the Legatii understand.

This, Caesar himself understands.

But I fear it took three near-revolutions before it dawned upon the new Governor General that this was no fantasy, no hearsay, but timeless unalterable fact!

I am not trying to provoke you (far from it!) and please forgive me if I seem repetitious and boring. But I must stress, again and again, the point that we will endure almost anything provided that it offends not against God's Honour and the dignity of our Spiritual Laws. Thus, painful though it may be, I am asking you, in all humility, to recollect those three most unfortunate "incidents" over which had not a more tactful attitude prevailed each time at the very last moment, the results would have been even more appalling in their consequence.

Firstly, it was explicitly laid down in the Treaty between Rome and Palestine that the Imperial Standards bearing GRAVEN IMAGES should never desecrate the Holy City by their presence. But the newly appointed Governor General, despite every warning, insisted on having these GRAVEN IMAGES trooped from their rightful resting place at Caesarea to the Antonia Palace in Jerusalem, thereby flaunting and mocking THE COMMANDMENT, an act never contemplated by your illustrious predecessors – their former Excellencies, Marcus Ambibulus, Amnius Rufus, or even Valerius Gratus.

Yet, when we made proper protest, you tried to deceive us by having the Standards trooped in, veiled and under cover of darkness. Because of this action, you may recall, there was a protest march all the way to Caesarea, not by members of the Sanhedrin (nor at their instigation) but by hundreds of common ordinary devout Jews who sat down outside your Palace for five days and five nights refusing to move until they received your undertaking that the Standards would be removed from Jerusalem. Again with little understanding (the obvious fault of the Colonial Office) you had your soldiers threaten them with their swords if they would not get up and disperse. But our People, who would rather die than see their Law profaned, bowed passively before your mighty cohorts, baring their necks inviting the swords to strike.

Hastily I laud Your Excellency's Statesmanship in ordering swords to be sheathed and in ordering the prompt return of the Standards to Caesarea!

Secondly, the unfortunate business of the golden shields in the Residency, inscribed with Caesar's Name coupled with that of the Governor General. Here, I must admit, it surely seemed strange to you that a mere *inscription* rather than a Graven Image should cause any offence against the First or Second COMMANDMENT. But our People are extremely sensitive (more so than you imagine) and had not yet forgotten the first incident. Such was the clamour of their protest that the entire Sanhedrin (along with all the princely sons of Herod Magnus, to wit – H.R.H. Prince Herod Antipas, our present King, H.R.H. Prince Herod-Philip, H.R.H. Prince Philip and H.R.H. Prince Herod) felt obliged to draw up a very respectful letter to Tiberius Caesar, begging him NOT to confer this great honour upon us, but to deny it. And He, of his gracious wisdom, and in fullest sympathy with our national conscience, so directed that the controversial shields be re-hung in the Temple of Augustus at Caesarea – thus once more averting a catastrophe.

Lastly, and with less happy ending, came the business of the municipal water supply. And to you, this must have seemed the least comprehensible! But it well illustrates the difficulties in governing the Province and the need for utmost tact in preserving the delicate harmony between our two Peoples.

An adequate supply of fresh water has always been a major problem in the Capital, more so in the summer months, and it was most laudable of the Governor General to have the Old Herodian Aqueduct cleaned and repaired, and to have the Old Siloan Tunnel cleared of silt and the masonry strengthened. Now, it was perfectly legal for you to debit the costs of these operations to the Temple Treasury Account, as agreed and laid down in the relevant Section of the "Tractate of the Shekalim" – Legal, but not very tactful!

Once again, the conscience of our people, ever mindful of our civil and religious rights, caused them to stage a large, peaceful and orderly protest march, with deplorable consequences. Now I am sure it could never have been Your Excellency or anyone remotely of his Entourage who gave the fatal Order. I am sure it must have been a stupid blunder on the part of the Riot Police. But the cruel fact remains; batons were drawn, shields were raised and several hundred devout and peaceful Jews were brutally clubbed to death.

Alas, all of this could so easily have been avoided had our lines of communication been more effective.

But now – a fourth and even more serious situation has arisen; one which, if not dealt with properly and correctly could have far more devastating results, even to the point of plunging the entire Province into Anarchy and Civil War. One single agitator, an Essene, fired with delusions of grandeur, has falsely and impiously proclaimed himself to be The MESSIAH and has publicly declared himself to be the Enemy of Caesar and of Rome, and that his intentions are to take over first the Province, then the whole Earth. Last night he was properly tried and convicted by Us for the unspeakable crime of abrogating unto himself the Sacred and Forbidden SECRET NAME (which I may not write). Yet, I am led to understand that there remains some hesitancy on your part to uphold our Law, under which Law he must surely die. It is not merely my own opinion, but an opinion shared by the whole Council of the Grand Sanhedrin that unless this man is punished *immediately*, the one thing both Rome and Judaea most dread will come to pass – and you know the consequences as well as I do.

Forgive me if I seem to labour the point or even to seem disrespectful. But what – what, I pray you – is the life of one malefactor when weighed against the lives and safety of our Whole Nation?

> Most Respectfully,
> *ANNAS BEN SETH*
> Former High Priest.
> Former Primate of all Israel.

GOVERNOR GENERAL'S MEMORANDVM

(I)   I am commanded by HIS EXCELLENCY, THE GOVER-
      NOR GENERAL OF THE PROVINCE OF IVDAEA
      to thank the Former High Priest, Annas, Ben Seth, for his
      kindly advice and for reminding him most graphically of
      those three "incidents" which only a turbulent and stiff-
      necked people could have brought upon themselves, or could
      ever wish to recall.

(II) HIS EXCELLENCY has ever regretted that his efforts to
      maintain the Capital with adequate water supplies should
      have been so grossly misunderstood, or that its inhabitants
      could have thought to question the propriety and correct-
      ness of *their own Tractate* when required to make payment for
      same.

(III) HIS EXCELLENCY, at the *repeated* request of the Former
      High Priest, forgives him for "interfering" and for "being
      frank".

C. S. SCIPIO
A.D.C. TO H.E.

TO: The Most Reverend Annas Ben Seth D.D.
    Former High Priest of Iervsalem
    Former Primate of All Israel, etc. etc. etc.

S. P. Q. R.

THE RESIDENCY, IERVSALEM

Date: *Idem.*

Dear Caiaphas,

Pray what more do you want? That I should crucify *your King*? I have scourged him and, to satisfy the mob, had him publicly displayed from the Rostrum of the Residency.

He has been more than adequately punished. Surely you can see for yourself that he is now a broken man?

However, I do begin to realize the highly complex nature of your religious and national sentiments which, as Procurator, it is my duty to respect and uphold.

Therefore, to satisfy the above and to appease your supporters I SHALL SUSTAIN AND UPHOLD YOUR CONVICTION, SENTENCING HIM ON EACH AND EVERY COUNT.

But – to satisfy the requirements of JUSTICE, I shall then immediately release him under the Passover Amnesty, thus demonstrating the Clemency of Caesar, the Unity of our Courts, and the solidarity and mutual understanding that exists between Rome and the Jewish Nation.

Hail Caesar!
P.P
Dictated but not signed by
H.E. The Governor General.

ps. Or would you rather have that Anarchist, Barabbas?

COUNCIL OF THE
GRAND SANHEDRIN

Re. Jesus of Nazareth

Your Excellency,

On behalf of the Council of The Grand Sanhedrin we thank you for sustaining and upholding our verdict, and for the sentiments of solidarity, understanding and sympathy which you so graciously expressed.

But why do you call him "our king"? we have no king but Caesar!!!

We also thank you for kindly remembering the traditional Passover Amnesty, and for offering us the choice of Jesus or Barabbas.

We, the two and seventy members of the Council of The Grand Sanhedrin have unanimously decided that you should release unto us, BARABBAS.

Hail Caesar!
CAIAPHAS JERUSALEM

S. P. Q. R.

THE RESIDENCY, IERVSALEM

Date: *Idem*

My Dear Caiaphas,

I cannot really believe you are serious! Barabbas is a revolutionary and an anarchist of the most dangerous and violent nature. Recently your own Courts (and mine) were satisfied beyond every reasonable doubt that here was the real leader and instigator behind the last series of riots, armed insurrections, bottle throwing, overturning and setting fire to vehicles, rampaging through the City and brutally assaulting the Riot Police, leading to the calling out of troops and multiple bloodshed.

Only last week we were congratulating ourselves that we had apprehended the real trouble-maker, and could possibly look forward to a little spell of peace in the immediate future. But to release him now would be madness. It would be as good as admitting to the rabble "It's all been a big mistake. We're terribly sorry. Barabbas is just a poor dear misguided boy who doesn't know any better and has apologized for being a nuisance."

Would you like me to pin a medal on him, and for good measure give him a Rehabilitation Grant from the Temple Treasury?

For God's sake, Caiaphas, come to your senses!!

Hail Caesar!
PONTIVS PILATVS

Your Excellency,

Now it is you who are getting a little overwrought. Our decision is neither foolish nor emotional as you would imply; but one of cold, reasoned logic. Weighed, one against the other, Jesus in the long run is by far the more dangerous of the two. Barabbas, popular among certain sections of the rabble, a thug, an opportunist and a brutal creature seeking only his personal aggrandizement, has caused both of us a lot of trouble, BUT HE CLAIMS NO MESSIAHSHIP. He is a down-to-earth violent revolutionary and, as recently proved, no match for the efficiency of the Xth Legion!

Very well then, we release him. He goes back to his old ways, starts up more trouble. So let him. Yes, I know you are going to say that it is a principle that any man released under the Passover Amnesty can never again be convicted on Capital Charges. But we have our ways and means. If it's not to be "Horaath Schaar" then it will be another. Leave that to us. But Jesus is a different matter. He claims spiritual power. He claims to be the Son of God. So he must be put to the supreme test. Now our Prophets have foretold certain signs by which the long-awaited Messiah may irrefutably be identified. I do not suppose you will have burdened yourself with study in depth of our racial "superstitions", but we take our Prophets seriously. And there is one thing upon which they have all agreed. And that is that the ultimate and irrefutable sign of the Messiah will be his immunity from, and triumph over, physical death.

Do you not see the point? He cannot die if he is the Messiah (not that I believe him for one instant), therefore on the cross, this very afternoon, his followers will witness the ultimate repudiation of his vain and blasphemous pretentions. The crowds will swarm to Golgotha, waiting, hoping, for a last-minute miracle, a divine intervention, a rescuing legion of angels. But it won't happen.

Why won't it happen? Because he's a fraud; and you know it and I know it!

But until he is put to death his following will continue to grow, becoming in its pacifism a graver menace than the calculable violence of Barabbas. But with Jesus dead, everything falls into ruin about their ears.

Pray do not think me a cruel man. Our Laws are merciful. He shall be given every last-minute chance to confess and repent to save his soul. Section 81 of the Act states that "if before or during execution the condemned shall admit their guilt and repent, they are certain of God's forgiveness, and their share in 'The Bosom of Abraham'". For this very reason, priests invariably attend each execution urging the dying sinner to final repentance and forgiveness.

In this particular case I shall detail some of our most experienced theologians and confessors to be present by way of a "Divine Probe". They will tirelessly (in relays if needs be) provoke him to "prove" that he is the Son of God, by coming down from the cross, and overcoming death as foretold in all the Messianic Prophecies. The lesson to our people will be more than salutary!

I trust we have explained ourselves and our reasons to your complete satisfaction.

> Hail Caesar!
> *CAIAPHAS JERUSALEM*

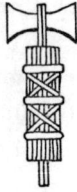

S. P. Q. R.

To His Grace, Ioseph Caiaphas, D.D.
High Priest of Iervsalem   Date: *Idem*
Primate of All Israel, etc. etc.

Your Grace,

Yes, you have explained yourselves with eminent lucidity! But you seem to have overlooked one minor point. Whatever its critics may say, Rome stands founded on Law, and Law (our Law) is rooted on Justice.

I cannot believe that the complex regulations of your Deity require you to pardon a murderer, and murder a pardoner. Thus, I shall not give you Barabbas. You shall have Jesus, and you shall treat him with gentleness, for he is in a state of shock after his flogging – on the justice of which I still entertain some profound reservations.

In my official capacity as Governor General, the supreme regional representative of Tiberius Claudius Caesar, and of the Senate and people of Rome, I hereby authorize and command that Jesus, son of Joseph, is released and shall go free without let or hindrance in accordance with the terms of the Passover Amnesty.

Hail Caesar!
PONTIVS PILATVS
BY IMPERIAL WARRANT
GOVERNOR GENERAL OF THE PROVINCE.

GOVERNOR GENERAL'S MEMORANDVM

FROM: A.D.C.　　　TO: H.E. The G.G.

Excellency,

　It's the H.P.J. (P.A.-I.) again. Shall I admit him?

NO! Tell him to put it in writing.　　　　　　*P.P.*

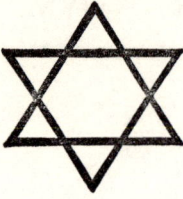

PALACE OF THE PRIMATE

EXTREME URGENCY
PRIVATE AND CONFIDENTIAL

Your Excellency,

Far be it for me to question your very good judgement, but have you just possibly noticed that there is a full-scale riot starting up in the street immediately below your windows? You may possibly also have observed that this riot is nothing more than the inevitable spontaneous reaction of my devout people to the announcement that the rabble-rouser rather than the blasphemer is to die.

I'm no longer thinking of myself, but of you! For this riot will rapidly get completely out of hand, and I regret there will be little the Temple Police can do to control it under the circumstances. Then what will happen if news of it reaches Rome? What will happen when it is established that the immediate cause was the aggrievement and distress caused to the ever loyal people of Jerusalem on learning that their Noble Governor General (for reason known only to himself) chose not only to set aside our Verdict and Sentence in a very serious religious matter, but to *ignore entirely* not one but *nine* treasonable and seditious charges against Caesar – counts to which I drew Your Excellency's urgent attention in my Judicial Memoranda but which charges (again for reasons best known only to you) Your Excellency saw fit to cast aside as of no importance.

We of the Sanhedrin tremble to think how Mighty Caesar will respond to such news! How are we going to help His Excellency explain Himself? How are we going to help His Excellency show cause to have pardoned a Traitor to Rome, thereby causing serious danger to Caesar's Peace, his Crown and Dignity? How are we going to make Mighty Caesar believe that the Governor General himself is not in fact a traitor to Rome?

130

Dear Pilatus, I beg of you, as an older man who has seen many turmoils and tumults, who has seen the rise and fall of many a noble Roman who has offended great Caesar, I beg of you – I implore you – do not throw away everything, your career, your wealth, your high position, even your life, merely on behalf of one misguided sorcerer, apostate and traitor!

Surely, surely, it is better that one obscure and unimportant man should die rather than the state be plunged into chaos, and that the fine career, not to say the physical well-being, of a most conscientious and well-intentioned Governor General be mortally endangered?

Believe me, my dear, my very dearest Pilatus, I have only your very best interest in my heart.

Hail Caesar!
CAIAPHAS JERUSALEM

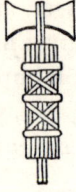

S. P. Q. R.

I wash my hands of the whole business!

If you wish to be guilty of the blood of an innocent, that is your affair. It is you, not I, who (according to your beliefs) shall one day have to render an account.

But, for the record, I want it made abundantly clear that whatsoever you do to him is according to your laws and no concern of Rome.

Take him therefore; take Jesus of Nazareth and do unto him what you will.

SIGNED WITH CAESAR'S SEAL

PONTIVS PILATVS,
BY IMPERIAL WARRANT
LORD PRESIDENT OF THE SVPREME COVRT
GOVERNOR GENERAL OF
THE PROVINCE OF IVDAEA

S. P. Q. R.

INDENT FORMA

UNIT: ARMOURY (Xth LEGION)   DATE a.d. III Nōn Apr.
A.U.C. DCCLXXXVI

ITEMS REQUIRED (Give Serial No's): Crosses, Crossbars, Execution Three (III)

WHEN REQUIRED: Immediate usage.

REASON REQUIRED: Execution, criminals, III

SIGNATURE OF INDENTOR: *Petronius Longinus*   RANK: *Cent.*

N.C.O. i/c Small Arms *Scipio Hex*   RANK: *R.S.M.*

CHECKED *V V*   *P.D.M.*   RANK: *Cpt.*

NOTES. *Poles to above already positioned on Golgotha.*
Measurements of each prisoner appended seperately as per pro-forma.

REMARKS: *None.*

S. P. Q. R.

STORES

FORMA DCCL/F/a
To be completed in Quadruplicate

INDENT FORMA

UNIT: A COHORT (Xth LEGION)   DATE: a.d. III Nōn Apr.

ITEMS REQUIRED (List separately): Grog ration, Execution Squad for I Officer, II N.C.O.'s and XXXII Other Ranks.

WHEN REQUIRED: Immediately

REASON REQUIRED (State clearly): Triple Execution III (Three) Criminals

NOTES: None

SIGNATURE OF INDENTOR: *Petronius Longinvs. Cent.*

REMARKS: *Double Grog Ration to be drawn for II Privates who have not been on Execution duties previously. Both soldiers are young and have only witnessed bloodshed during sword drill.*

P. Longinvs. Cent.

134

S. P. Q. R.

SENTENCE OF DEATH

NAME   Barabbas

OFFENCE(S)   I.   Armed Robbery with violence.

            II.   Causing Grievous Bodily Harm.

            III. Armed Insurrection, Causing Death to Divers
                  Persons.

            IV.   Plotting the Assassination of High Personages,
                  including Senior Members of The Council of
                  the Grand Sanhedrin.

            V.   Conspiracy against the State.

            VI.   XII Other Counts by his own admission,
                  taken into Consideration.

SENTENCE   Death By Crucifixion.

DATE   LIV A.U.C. DCCLXXXVI

                          SIGNED:
                            PONTIVS PILATVS

                          BY IMPERIAL WARRANT
                          GOVERNOR GENERAL OF
                          THE PROVINCE OF IVDAEA

*Granted Free Pardon in accordance with Passover Amnesty granted by Popular
Referendum at request of Sanhedrin.*

CANCELLED

FROM   GENERAL OFFICER COMMANDING Xth and
XIIth LEGIONS

CONFIDENTIAL

REGIMENTAL ORDER NO CXV/VI/A

(CONFIDENTIAL ORDER RESTRICTED TO OFFICERS ONLY)

The following CONFIDENTIAL ORDER is to be read and studied by ALL officers attendant upon or i/c Executions.

SUBJECT   *"Execution by the Cross"* (Methods and Procedure).

(I)   DEFINITION   A form of execution whereby the convicted body is affixed to a wooden cross causing death to take place from one or more of a number of reasons.

(II)   PURPOSE   To instil fear and respect for Lawful Authority. It is extremely painful and causes maximum terror both to those so condemned and to onlookers. It is an excellent preservative for Law and Order.

(III)   DETERRENT   The disquieting spectacle of a Public Crucifixion is the most effective deterrent and warning to any other would-be malefactors. Therefore it should always be conducted with maximum publicity; preferably immediately prior to or during a major feastday or public holiday, thereby ensuring its observance by the greatest possible number of spectators. To this end, skill is required for its effective operation and the control of its Duration.

(IV)   DURATION   Unlike most other methods of execution the duration can be prolonged or shortened at will according to the method and procedures selected by the Officer-in-Charge of Execution. An experienced officer can protract the death agonies for more than a day and a night. Or he can terminate them at will by selecting from the Methods and Procedures described in (V/A) and (V/B).

(V) ## METHODS AND PROCEDURES

(V/A) Longer, but less painful

In this method the condemned is affixed by the hands and feet by means of ropes. After hanging by the hands for ten minutes violent cramps attack the lungs and thorax making breathing extremely difficult and painful. This can only be relieved by alternating the weight between the hands and the feet until the condemned becomes too exhausted to continue. At this point the thorax seizes in a distended position and air can no longer be drawn into the lungs. Death follows swiftly, through suffocation.

In the case of healthy men, the above may last up to forty-eight hours. In exceptional cases it has been known to continue for three days and nights.

TERMINATION   The above can be determined at any time by the simple process of breaking both legs, leaving the weight of the body supported entirely from the arms. Asphyxiation follows within minutes.

(V/B) Shorter, but more painful

In this method, when it is desirable to cause death within six hours, the hands and feet are affixed to the wood by means of long nails (Types E. or G/I. proving most suitable).

Nails must NOT, repeat NOT, be driven into the palms of the hands or they will tear out of the soft flesh as soon as they take the full weight of the body. They must be driven through the thick part of the wrist and care must be taken to ensure that they have passed between the small gap in the wrist bones.

If this is done correctly, the fist will immediately clench in a locked spasm owing to penetration of the Median Nerve. Officers will watch for this spasm as it is the sign that nails have been correctly driven. Failing which it is recommended to withdraw nails and to recommence procedure.

The Left Foot should be crossed over the Right and a single Long Nail (G/I or G/II) driven through both insteps to a depth of at least four inches into the wood.

137

As with (V/A) above, violent cramps rapidly seize the thorax, distending it, and making exhalation progressively more difficult. Had the convicted no other support than the nails death would very soon take place.

(V/C) SEDILLA, FUNCTION OF AND NECESSITY FOR,

To obviate rapid death a small support, seat or sedilla is placed directly beneath feet and/or buttocks (depending on size and weight of convicted) so that the weight can be transferred to it from time to time allowing normal lung-function. After, but not before, the feet have been nailed the sedilla must be inserted and pushed up beneath them and fastened securely to give the requisite support.

It is MOST IMPORTANT the sedilla be properly and accurately positioned or it will fail to give the requisite support, causing premature death. Conversely it must not be too "comfortable" or the death struggles will be inordinately minimized.

If a sedilla is placed beneath the buttocks, it is necessary to secure that part of the body loosely by ropes or it will slide off the sedilla during contractions again causing premature suffocation.

(VI) HOLES, NAIL Holes for the nails should be drilled in advance. By reason of this it is most essential that the convicted be properly and accurately measured, or unsatisfactory results will ensue. In cases of multiple execution, each cross should therefore be marked with a small sign or number identifying it with the intended occupant.

(VII) PROCESSION, THE A very important part of the deterrent lies in the procession to the execution area, wherein further public exposure and mockery is made available to the convicted. During this, each malefactor is required to carry the cross-bar and/or the pole, depending on his physical ability at the time.

If he has previously undergone scourging as part of the Sentence, he is seldom able to carry more than the cross-bar. In many cases he is too weakened even to accomplish this duty, whereupon it is expedient and lawful to imp an onlooker for the task.

Should any onlooker, on being so impressed, refuse to comply he may be dealt with summarily as the officer i/c sees fit.

(VIII)   <u>DEATH</u>   Once the convicted has been properly secured by either Procedures (V/A) or (V/B) above, the nails and/or other fastenings will be inspected and approved by the officer i/c before the base of the pole is inserted in the ground in the pre-prepared hole. After raising to vertical position, wedges will be driven into the remaining aperture of the hole to ensure uprightness and stability.

When Procedure (V/A) (Rope fastenings) have been opted for the convicted will suffer less initial pain but his spasms will be of much longer duration.

When Procedure (V/B) (Nails) have been opted for, the convicted (as in V/A) can relieve his lungs only by taking the weight off his hands and placing the full weight of his body on his pierced feet. This <u>inescapable</u> shifting of the weight back and forth from hands to feet must continue for as long as he has the will to survive, or suffocation must take place. The convicted continually fights and gasps for breath, and each breath is taken at the expense of <u>excruciating alternations of pain</u> between hands and feet.

As with (V/A) death can be determined at any time at the discretion of the officer i/c by the simple expedient of breaking both legs, so that he can no longer avail himself of their support or of the support of the Sedilla. After the legs have been broken death follows almost immediately.

(IX)   <u>DEATH, SIGNS OF</u>   When death takes place the lungs are locked in a cramp in a fully distended position which is easily recognizable. To double-check death has taken place, the Officer i/c is recommended to pierce the lung cavity. If a watery fluid mixed with traces of blood issues forth it is a sure sign that the lung has filled with liquid and death already ensued.

(X)   <u>GENERAL</u>   It will readily be seen from the above that the simple perfection of this type of execution lies in the fact that not only the agonies and intensity of pain are largely under the control of the officer i/c, but also their duration. As executional methods go, none has yet been bettered for its simplicity of operation, its ease of maintaining full control, and its devastating effect upon witnesses.

As a force for good, inexperienced officers and officers new to these operations should be fortified in the sure knowledge that for every felon crucified an estimated hundred witnesses are so impressed by the salutary spectacle that any incipient thoughts of crime or sedition are banished from their minds – often permanently.

They can therefore feel assured that while crucifying one, they are saving ninety-nine from a similar fate, and should take heart accordingly as public benefactors.

(XI)   <u>PROCEDURES, POST EXECUTIONAL</u>

(A) On death being established, body (bodies) will be taken down and buried without honour in the quicklime pit which has usually been prepared in the area most adjacent.

(B) This having been done, crosses will be dismantled, the site will be left tidy, and the squad will return to barracks.

(XII)   <u>MEMENTOES</u>   There has been some confusion regarding memento-seeking by onlookers or relatives of the convicted. To clarify this: there is no inherent objection to this being done as these mementoes will serve as an added reminder (and deterrent) of the Absolute and Undefiable Power of Rome.

However, in regions such as this Province, bearing in mind the acute timber shortage, crosses, when dismantled, should be thoroughly cleaned and returned to Q.M. Stores (or Armoury as the case may be per unit) for future Usage. Nails, however, if bent or damaged may be freely distributed at the discretion of the officer i/c.

Cont/VI   (FROM G.O.C. Xth and XII)

THE ABOVE CONFIDENTIAL ORDER WILL BE CAREFULLY STUDIED AND MEMORIZED BY ALL OFFICERS WHO WILL SIGN IT BELOW AND ON THE FOLLOWING PAGES AS HAVING BEEN READ AND UNDERSTOOD.

(signed)

PAVLVS GRATVS TEMERIVS

General Officer Commanding
Xth and XIIth Legions

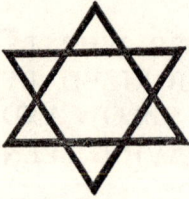

PALACE OF
THE PRIMATE

URGENT BY HAND

~~UNACCEPTABLE
RETURN
TO SENDER~~

Excellency!
   You *cannot* put that! i.e. "IESVS OF NAZARETH KING OF
THE IEWS" It's bad enough in Greek and Latin, but in Hebrew
too! Words fail me. It's an insult to my whole people.
   Could you not change this offensive inscription to: "IESVS OF
NAZARETH WHO <u>SAID</u> HE WAS KING OF THE IEWS"?
Or, better still, "WHO FALSELY CLAIMED TO BE 'KING'
OF THE IEWS".
   At very least, put the word: "KING" in large – **very large**
inverted commas. Though I doubt the mob would appreciate the
subtlety.

Respectfully
CAIAPHAS JERUSALEM

What I have written I have written. P.P.

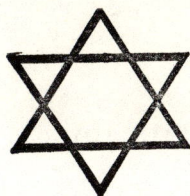

COUNCIL OF THE
GRAND SANHEDRIN

Eve of Pesach.

Your Excellency,

In accordance with Section 23 of the Act it is (may we respectfully remind you?) required that the bodies of any executed felons be removed from the gibbets prior to the commencement of the Sabbath.

We therefore request Your Excellency that in the case of the three malefactors at present undergoing crucifixion that their legs be broken immediately so as to accelerate death by suffocation, and that their bodies be promptly disposed of, without honour, in accordance with the above Act.

We have the Honour to Remain,
Your Excellency's Most Obt and Mch Oblgd Svts
NATHAN BEN SETH
Per Pro The Sanhedrin.

S. P. Q. R.

FORMA IIA

GVBERNATORIAL AVDIENCE.   Svpplication Forma

NAME OF SUPPLICANT
Joseph of Arimathea

REASONS FOR SEEKING AVDIENCE (State your reasons, clearly, concisely, and respectfully. Fill in all three copies. One to be handed to Capt. of Guard; one to A.D.C. to H.E., and one to Private Secretary; respectively.

I most earnestly request I see you IMMEDIATELY. Please cut the formalities as it is almost the third hour and I want your permission to obtain custody of the body of Jesus of Nazareth. Burial rites must all be completed before the Passover which is nearly upon us. I shall not detain you more than a few moments . . . Please! I beg of you . . .

Most respectfully,
JOSEPH OF ARIMATHEA

FOR OFFICIAL VSE ONLY

	GRANTED	NOT GRANTED	DEFERRED
***	√	×	×

	APPROVED	NOT APPROVED	SIGNED
*	√	×	*RPM*

GOVERNOR GENERAL'S MEMORANDVM

VRGENT

The OFFICER-in-CHARGE, EXECUTIONS, is to report to the Person of The Governor-General IMMEDIATELY

Before leaving Execution Area he is to establish **positively** the deaths of the three felons concerned (using approved Procedure laid down in CONFIDENTIAL Regimental Order No. CXV/XI/A Sections QV/A), (V/B), (X)), paying particular attention in the case of Iesvs of Nazareth.

(Signed)
C. S. SCIPIO
A.D.C. TO H.E. THE G.G.

S. P. Q. R.

FORMA XII/IV/A

TO   H.E. The Governor General

FROM   Petronivs Longinvs, Centvrion, A Cohort. Xth Legion.

SVBJECT   EXECVTION REPORT

DATE   a.d. II Nōn Apr. A.V.C. DCCLXXXVI

COPIES TO.   (I) G.O.C. Xth Legion. (II) Registrar of Births, Deaths and Marriages; (III) Public Prosecutor; (IV) Church and Ecclesiastical Court Authorities

Sir,

I beg to submit my report re. Execution of yesterday's date of two thieves and one public agitator (names appended separately).

I have already given Your Excellency a verbal report when summoned by Your Command from the place where I was conducting said Executions (in the proper manner as laid down in Emperor's Regulations and in Regimental Standing Orders) to discuss immediate removal of the body of the public agitator at the request of the Hon. Joseph of Arimathea.

Your Excellency questioned me intently in the presence of the Hon. J. Arimathea as to whether the execution of the agitator had actually been completed and death taken place. I replied that death had indeed occurred and Your Excellency showed some surprise that it had taken place within such short a period (three hours). So that the three bodies might be removed, as is required by Law, before the onset of the Sabbath, we had adopted standard Procedure of breaking legs so that death might follow swiftly by reason of suffocation. When we came to the public agitator it appeared that death had in fact already taken place. To test this, I pierced his side using a Spear (General Usage) whereupon blood and lymph flowed briefly from the ensuing wound, indicating the lungs had ceased to function. No sign of life was evident.

On receiving Your Excellency's Summons and instructions I hastened back to Golgotha and ordered my Squad to remove all three bodies, starting, as ordered, with that of the public agitator. As the nails were removed and laid on the ground, the earth tremors commenced causing considerable speculation and agitation among the onlookers. Body was then delivered as per Your Orders to Hon. J. Arimathea and other relatives of same.

I beg to submit to Your Notice that all details of above executions were correctly carried out in accordance with Approved Procedures as per relevant Secs and Subsecs in Emps: Regs: and S.O.'s.

I have the Honour to be,
Sir,
Your Excellency's Most Obt Svt
PETRONIVS LONGINVS
Officer i/c Execution Squad.

UNIT   A. COHORT. Xth LEGION

TO   General Officer Commanding Xth Legion

FROM   P. Longinvs, Centvrion.

SUBJECT Report on and explanation for my conduct during execution of Iesvs of Nazareth.

DATE   a.d. XIII Kal. Apr. A.V.C. DCCLXXXVI

Sir,

I have the honour to report that, following criticism and reprimand concerning my conduct during and after above execution, I admit that I uttered, within earshot of many non-nationals, the words: "Truly this man was a Son of God."

Sir, my reasons for doing so are as follows:
The behaviour and demeanour of this prisoner was most unusual to say the very least. Unlike every other convict it has been my duty to crucify, this man did not once curse, swear, nor use obscene language. SIR, every felon I have known to suffer this fate invariably makes the most of his final opportunity to defy authority by blaspheming and raining curses upon the Squad for so long as breath lasts him. We ignore and accept this as an inevitable part of the unpleasantness associated with these specialized duties.

But even during the driving in of the nails, the prisoner in question bore himself with extreme fortitude. He looked at me steadily, not with the usual mixture of anguish and hatred but with deepest compassion. He prayed, saying, "Father, forgive them, they know not what they do."

At this my men were momentarily taken aback, but continued to carry out their task without being called to order. But I was most perturbed by prisoner's remark; all the more so, considering his very weakened condition caused by his recent scourging. During the execution procession he fell three times under the weight of the cross-bar, so that I impressed a bystander to render assistance (as I am entitled to do) same bystander being one by name of Simon Cyrenivs who complained at the outset, but very soon appeared to show every sign of great happiness, as if this humiliating experience and strenuous exertion was in fact a most enjoyable task. That, Sir, is the first thing that differed from the norm.

The second is that during one halt, a number of women in the jostling mob began lamenting and weeping over the prisoner who turned to them with tears in his own eyes, saying: "Daughters of Jerusalem, don't weep for me. Weep for yourselves and your children." And I realized that despite his pain and exhaustion, his tears were caused by the spectacle of their grief. By this time, Sir, I had come to suspect that he was a very unusual man.

My uneasiness increased further when a woman, who gave her name as Veronica, broke through the Guard and gently wiped his face with a good quality linen hankerchief. Prisoner thanked her most courteously as she was removed to prevent further hold-ups. Which having been done, we proceeded to Golgotha and affixed said bodies to their respective crosses, as per regulations.

When the bodies had been affixed and had settled down a bit, the crowds in attendance became very thick as many interested spectators had accompanied the Squad; their numbers increasing all the time. The crowds seemed aggressive and hostile toward the prisoner Iesvs, so I took the precaution of mounting a cordon to keep them back from the gibbets, while permitting the Chaplains and Confessors to come close to him, as they had expressed the desire to question him further, saying it was their duty to test his alleged messiahship to the bitter end, and also to give him a chance of last-minute repentance.

The padres questioned him continually, e.g.: "If you are the Christ and King of Israel, come down off your cross and we'll all believe you." And, e.g.: "You said you are the Son of God. You trust in God? All right, so now let God come and deliver you." But when nothing happened the crowds became abusive (disappointed, I would think) hurling insults and abuse at him ceaselessly and without pity. But completely ignoring the other two felons who did not merit or attract their attention. Typical of their cries were: "You saved others. Now save yourself." and: "Now work a miracle! Come down off that cross!" and "He said he was the Son of God. Let God come and save him! *Then* we'll all believe" etc. etc. and other epithets too offensive to be included in this report. Even members of my Squad became affected and began joining in the general mockery, making frequent reference to the inscription placed above his head, by Command of His Excellency, to the effect that Iesvs was the King of the Iews; in that they shouted: "If you're King of the Iews, let's see you save yourself!" (I might respectfully add, Sir, that this inscription had caused great offence among certain sections of the native community.) Things came to such a pass that I reinforced the cordon, fearing a breakthrough, and pushed back the crowds a little, for I feel that it is right even for a convict to die in some sort of peace if possible.

To quieten my men, I permitted those not on cordon to divide up the spoils, such as they were, each man to take some garment or souvenir of the deceased. But as those of the Nazarene were of fine quality and woven all in one piece, I let my men indulge in a little gambling, throwing dice for its possession. This pacified them somewhat. But those on cordon grumbled until called to order. Despite my actions the crowd continued to evince hostility and became ever more abusive, even infecting one of the dying criminals. He had been yelling his head off with the cramps, but found it in him to shout: "If you're the Christ, for God's sake save yourself and save *us too!*" At which point another strange occurrence took place. The other thief turned and rebuked him with words to the effect: "We're here dying for our sins. Aren't you afraid of God? We've got what we deserved. But this man here's done nothing wrong."

This seemed to quieten him, though he continued cursing intermittently till the end. But meanwhile the first thief turned to Iesvs and asked rather piteously: "Dear Lord, please remember me when you come into your Kingdom!"

And Iesvs looked at him, very kindly, very reassuring, and answered: "Today, I promise you, truly you will be with me in Paradise." Most unusual I thought.

It was about this time (the ninth hour) that it suddenly began to get dark, and continued getting darker until the earthquake took place. By that time, some of the crowds had dispersed, while other people had gone away bored, others again had gone disappointed that no last-minute miracle had taken place in the form of a spectacular escape for this legendary wonder-worker. I hasten to add, Sir, that had I believed these reports for one instant I would have mounted my entire Cohort to obviate any such miracle.

Some of the next of kin now came forward (which I allowed). The Nazarene looked down compassionately on his weeping mother who was clutching the base of the cross. He called to one who I believe is called Ioannes, saying: "She is your mother now. Look after her for me." And to her he said: "This is your son," referring to said Ioannes.

Meanwhile the darkness got worse until we could hardly see a thing. But we heard Iesvs call out: "I'm so thirsty." So I sent a man stumbling off at the double to fill a sponge with vinegar and pain deadeners which prisoner drank through a reed most gratefully. I continually stress prisoner's attitude, Sir, not to be repetitious, but so that you may perceive for yourself how unusual was his behaviour and how unnerving to a veteran executioner who had never witnessed the like of it before.

Then, shortly after he had taken the drink Iesvs lifted up his head and cried aloud. There seems to be some slight confusion as to his actual words and I'm afraid my knowledge of local dialect is not perfect. But some say he called to Elias. Others say he called upon his God. But then the words: "Eli" and "Eloi" are very similar and could easily be confused. "Why have you deserted me?" he cried. Then a great calm seemed to come over him as if he knew the end had come. He looked upwards saying: "Father into your hands I commit my spirit." Then with a very loud cry: "It is finished!" he died.

Then the earthquake took place and I admit I was frightened for the first time since the execution began. I admit that by now the whole thing had completely unnerved me. Not only me, but some of the bystanders as well. A dreadful feeling of guilt (something I hadn't known in years) overcame me. Yes, Sir, I freely admit that my conduct became most unmilitary. I fell on my knees in the sight of all, prayed aloud, and told my entire Squad that we had crucified an innocent man, a saint, the Son of God. I freely admit that I said he was the Son of God, and so help me, I am still of that opinion!

In view of the above I humbly submit myself, Sir, to the judgement of my Superior Officers, respectfully asking that the very unusual and extenuating and harrowing circumstance be borne in mind.

I have the Honour to be, Sir,
Your Most Obt, and Hbl Svt
PETRONIVS LONGINVS
Centvrion

S. P. Q. R.

ARMOVRY

TO   Officer i/c Executions, Centvrion P. Longinvs.

FROM   Sgt. Mjr. i/c Armoury.

SUBJECT   Spear G.S. Loss of.

DATE   a.d. VIII Id. Apr.

Sir,
    I have the honour to report that one (I) Spear, General Service was not returned to Armoury after the executions on a.d. IV Nōn. Apr. Inquiries indicate it was purloined by some by-standers, Sir. Sir, to whom do we debit this said item, sir?

I have the Honour to be
Sir,
Yr Obt Svt
JULIVS PETRVS   S.M.

TO. S.M. i/c Armoury.

Enquiries are in progress. You will be advised as to defrayment and replacement.

P. LONGINVS.
Centvrion.

S. P. Q. R.

FORMA B/XII/cc/II

SPECIAL REQVEST FORMA

NATVRE OF REQVEST
Special Guard.

PVRPOSE
To guard the tomb of the executed Iesvs of Nazareth against grave robbers.

REASON
The Above Iesvs and his followers have proclaimed he would rise from the tomb within a period of three days, and it is suspected that an attempt may be made to open it and remove body from same. The tomb should therefore be under twenty-four hour Guard for at least three days.

NAME(S) OF REQVESTOR(S)

B. NATHAN
p.p. The Sanhedrin

/ APPROVED	/ NOT APPROVED	/ DEFERRED /
√	×	×

FOR OFFICIAL VSE ONLY.

One Company under the Command of a Centurion to be on XXIV hour Guard until further notice.

Seven wax seals impressed with the Gubernatorial Seal to be securely affixed to Tomb Entry.

Severe penalties to be imposed for unauthorized removal or tampering with same.

Q. LINÆVS
Adjvtant

GOVERNOR GENERAL'S MEMORANDVM

Midnight *Idem*

My loyal and trusty Scipio,

It has been one of *those* days!!!

Pray see to it that neither Her Excellency nor myself are disturbed again during the remainder of the Passover. We are both exhausted!

P.P.

S. P. Q. R.

THE FOLLOWING SECTION IS CLASSIFIED

TOP SECRET

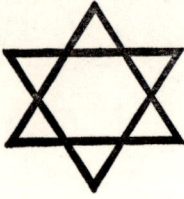

PALACE OF
THE PRIMATE

MOST URGENT.

"E Y E S   O N L Y"   THE   GOVERNOR   GENERAL

Re. Jesus of Nazareth   Date   Nisan 16

Excellency,

In the early hours of this morning, certain persons, presumably followers of the late Nazarene, apparently introduced drugs into the water ration of the Guard mounted (at our insistence) on the tomb belonging to Joseph of Arimathea, with disastrous results.

Whilst the soldiers were in an unconscious condition the party, which must have numbered at least six persons, contrived to prise open the monument and steal the body of the above executed felon.

Did we not strongly and repeatedly advise your noble self on the dangers and undesirability of allowing this felon the *completely irregular* privilege of normal burial? The fire or the quicklime pit are good enough for normal criminals so that we are still unable to understand your lenience in allowing this most unfortunate exception to be made in this instance; albeit, despite the strong influence of the Arimathea pressure group.

The point is this! – IMMEDIATE recovery of the body is now essential. Every possible agent must be impressed to locate it so that it can be shown and presented to the people dead – well and truly dead. For who knows the consequences of failure in this respect? His crazy claim of resurrection will most certainly be used to continue and perpetuate his cult.

The body MUST be found.

CAIAPHAS   JERUSALEM

156

S. P. Q. R.

THE RESIDENCY, IERVSALEM

Pridie Id. Apr.

Your Grace,

I was hauled out of my bath by a breathless messenger bearing your "EYES ONLY" missive. Frankly I think you are becoming just a trifle overwrought by the entire business. Don't take it so personally! I have already been informed of the body-snatching through Military Intelligence who are taking the necessary counter-measures. Furthermore, the Duty Guard have already admitted to falling asleep at their posts and are being dealt with by their Superior Officer.

I know he got your gall (Jesus I mean) by his presumptuous challenge to Established Spiritual Authority (yours!) so that to please you and the Sanhedrin I, Pilatus, not without many misgivings, upheld your sentence and permitted YOU to carry out the Supreme Penalty.

J. Arimathea is an old friend of mine, and I felt the least I could do was to allow him to give his relative a decent burial (I am empowered to waive regulations so do not challenge me further) and I have absolutely no regrets at conceding him this small courtesy.

However, you may take comfort to know that "Intelligence" had long previously planted a most reliable Agent into the ranks of the Nazarene Party, and are keeping me fully informed as to developments. I agree with you that the body must be found, and found it shall be to obviate further disorders.

Per Pro H.E. THE GOVERNOR GENERAL.

C.S.C.

Dictated by His Excellency
while dressing and signed
in absentio.

POST SCRIPTUM. I have re-read your letter more carefully and am putting the Duty Guard to "The Question". They will tell the whole truth. They invariably do!

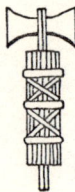

S. P. Q. R.

a.d. VII Idus Apriles.

PRIVATE AND CONFIDENTIAL

Most Revered Primate,

With deepest regret I have to inform you that you have lost your money!

Did you honestly believe you could bribe serving Members of His Imperial Majesty's Army of Occupation and get away with it? Oh yes, I know you will promptly claim Ecclesiastic Immunity from any proceedings I may consider bringing against your Sacred Personage, therefore I shall rest content by informing you that you had *no need whatsoever to bribe* my soldiers into pretending they were drugged.

They were!

The very urgency and tone of your letter made me suspect it might be advantageous to question the defaulters further. The mere sight of the "Apparrati" is often sufficiently fearful to save us the unpleasant necessity of having to use it. To a man they confessed that they had most willingly accepted your bribe – and in good conscience too. For what they did not tell you were the peculiar hallucinatory properties of the drugs which (I agree with you) were obviously introduced into their water ration prior to mounting guard.

For your notes and interest, it appears that each man experienced almost identical hallucinations. Being a religious man you will doubtless understand this far better than I – Their garbled, frightened, yet curiously consistent stories indicate they "saw angels", or some other species of celestial beings, descend from the sky, paralyse the Guard, and open the tomb.

The Forensic Department is now investigating, but I suspect it may be difficult to obtain much worthwhile evidence from blood

158

tests, for I am reliably informed that the quantities of drug required to produce these pseudo-spiritual experiences are minimal.

However, I am in firm agreement with you that the body must be found – the sooner the better. Following which I trust we shall hear no more of this nonsense.

In the meanwhile I have confiscated your *very* generous "offerings" and have donated them to the Garrison Temple of Jupiter (Caesarea).

Hail Caesar!
PONTIVS PILATVS

BY IMPERIAL WARRANT
GOVERNOR GENERAL OF THE
PROVINCE OF IVDAEA

METEOROLOGICAL OFFICE
CAESAREA

a.d. V Id. Apr.
A.U.C. DCCLXXXVI

SEISMOGRAPHIC REPORT

The Earthquake that took place at the ninth hour last Friday (a.d. IV Non. Apr) was of medium intensity, with Epicentre in the region of the Hill of Golgotha. The shock wave passed eastwards through the Temple Area of the City and westwards to the sea, following upon an unusually heavy overcast sky of such severity that lamps had to be lit in many parts.

DAMAGE ASSESSMENT

Damage to the City was fortunately not severe, but the huge lintel to the Portico of the Temple fractured and collapsed; and it is reported that the Veil of the Temple was torn in two, thus exposing the "Holy of Holies" to unauthorized viewing, to the considerable distress of the Religious Authorities, some of whom chose to see a connection between this purely natural event and the execution of another self-styled prophet which took place concurrently.

There was also some damage to Mt Zion Cemetery causing tombs to split open and their contents to be spilled, giving rise to a popular rumour that "the dead were rising from their graves". The Cemetery Supt reports that the "newly risen dead" are being replaced in their accustomed resting places with maximum alacrity! But because of the public alarm, and to prevent the spread of unfounded fears and supersitition, we have examined the report of the Centurion i/c Executions (a man, needless to say of no geological nor scientific learning) who informed us that the earth tremors commenced at the precise moment he laid the nails on the ground which had been used in the case of the self-styled prophet. There is not the slightest scientific evidence that would tend to suggest that this small extra weight upon the Earth's surface could have any such triggering effect, and it would be gross superstition to attribute any least connection whatever between the two totally unrelated events. No further major tremors are expected in the immediate foreseeable future.

Signed

M.B.S.

ASSISTANT

MOUNT ZION CEMETERY

Nisan 19, 3794

REPORT ON VANDALISM, NISAN 16

I, the undersigned, hereby certify that on the night of Nisan 16 certain persons unknown broke into and entered a Tomb at Golgotha, the property of the Hon. Joseph Arimathea G.C.S. recently erected by him as his Family Mausoleum.

The tomb in question had been opened and the door-stone, though sealed, deposited four yards eighteen inches (approx.) from the tomb entrance.

The remains of the Deceased, interred therein only on Nisan 14, have been purloined, though the funereal garments remain intact and undisturbed.

The grave-spoilers must have acted with utmost skill and daring, for there was a special Guard mounted throughout the night consisting of a Detachment from D Cohort, Xth Legion, under the Command of a Centurion, which we are so informed had been posted on direct orders from the Praetorium.

In view of these precautions we are at a loss to offer explanation as to how the robbery could have been effected.

Signed
JOSHUA BEN COHEN
(Superintendent of Cemeteries)

FORENSIC DEPARTMENT

PRAETORIVM

IERVSALEM

PROVINCE OF IVDAEA

Forma C/D/III/c

Ref: IC/PP/I

TO   Officer i/c Military Intelligence

SUBJECT   Blood tests to Duty Guard (Special Picket)
Nights of Nisan 14/16 (incl.)

REPORT

Blood samples taken from the above guards while undergoing
questioning revealed no traces of drugs, other than the normal
alcoholic content consistent with guards on night duty.

Q.L.

Assistant (LABS)

I'BRAM, I'BRAM, NATHAN, JACOB, SONS & CO.
(MORTICIANS) LTD

Nisan 25 3794

Ref. IM/JA/N   (*Idibus Apr. A, DCCLXXXVI*)

To The Captain of the Guard,
The Praetorium,
Antonia Barracks,
Jerusalem 1.

Most Honoured Sir,

At your Esteemed Command, we hasten to submit herewith our report about the disgraceful act of sacrilege on the night of Nisan 16.

In all our long and reputable experience as the capital's Leading Morticians we have never before come across a more shocking and disgraceful, nay, wanton, case of body-snatching.

We had very recently completed a small but very tasteful Mausoleum for the family of our long standing and most illustrious client, the Hon. Joseph of Arimathea, and we were sorely distressed to learn of his recent bereavement. We were however, somewhat shocked to ascertain the nature of death suffered by his Loved One. But fortunately for us, the friends of the family made their own arrangements re. The Interrment, and were allowed the usage of said tomb consequent upon a Special Dispensation for Burial, graciously granted by H.E. The Governor General.

The Mausoleum, so defiled, was one of our most recent works and we were extremely proud of it. The workmanship is of the highest quality, and we were greatly relieved to learn that it has suffered little or no irreparable damage. We have already submitted estimates for its repair which we trust will be found very reasonable as we are allowing our Esteemed Client the full benefit of the Seven Year Guarantee that accompanies all our products.

The door-stone alone weighs nearly two tons and was meticulously socketed and morticed to an accuracy of plus or minus one-tenth of an inch. We have carefully examined it for chisel marks and have found none. Nor do crowbars or tools of any kind (essential to prise it from its setting) appear to have been utilized. Thus, we are inclined to the opinion that the only manner by which said door-stone could have been removed and deposited a number of yards distant would be by gaseous pressure building up within the tomb, possibly leading to an explosion, allied doubtless to subsidence following the earthquake of Nisan 14, on which occasion no small number of tombs suffered varying degrees of damage.

But whilst the gaseous outrush might account for the displacement of said door-stone and for the unconscious condition of the Duty Guard, it would not be entirely consistent with the condition of the funereal garments which showed no sign of fouling through rapid bodily decomposition. We have most thoroughly examined said funereal garments (prior to their disappearance) and remain at a loss to comprehend by what means the Body could have been extricated therefrom, as they remained completely undisturbed, fully wrapped and correctly folded, giving the curious appearance as if they had suddenly collapsed inwardly upon themselves, retaining the outline of the Body previously within them. The Veil (headpiece), likewise, remains correctly folded and in place, though set a short distance apart.

We beg to be allowed to restate that this was one of our very finest monuments, of the highest quality workmanship, and we are deeply distressed and aggrieved at the sacrilege it has suffered. Trusting and hoping most sincerely that through your good offices you will swiftly bring the vandals to the justice they so richly deserve.

Assuring you of our very best attention at all times.

We have the Honour, Sir, to Remain,
Yr Most Hbl & Obt Svts
NATHAN B. SPINGOLD
Director
For and on Behalf of I'Bram I'Bram, Nathan,
Jacob, Sons & Co. Ltd

CONFIDENTIAL

HR III CHAMBERLAIN

Nisan 22 3794.

TO. Director, "Military Intelligence"
The Praetorium, Antonia Barracks, Jerusalem 1

FROM H.M. Chamberlain.

His Majesty, King Herod Antipas, is deeply concerned about increasing reports re. an alleged "resurrection" of the recently executed Jesus of Nazareth.

These reports have been confirmed to His Majesty's satisfaction by Mrs Joanna Chusa, wife of his Chief Steward, who swears by the altar of the temple that she and two other women found the tomb empty and were there confronted by an "angelic manifestation".

She furthermore swears that one of her companions, Miriam of Magdala later returned to the tomb where she encountered the person of the late Nazarene, apparently in the fullness of health.

His Majesty requires *immediate confirmation or denial* of the above alleged event, as the case may be.

If the report should be positive he wishes to know your proposals for dealing with same.

D.L.

HRIII

My Dear Pontius,

Thank you for coming so promptly to see Us and for giving Us your many reassurances. We think your proposed lines of action should be satisfactory and We are most relieved to learn you have first-class agents dealing with the case.

We quite agree that it is now in all our interests to combine forces and to suppress this monstrous conspiracy before it takes root and flowers; despite our previous differences let Us now forget the past and extend the hand of friendship.

You do think it's only a human conspiracy, don't you, and not a genuine rising from the dead? First John, now Jesus. I confess a cold fear is upon Me such as I have never known before – not even in those fearful days when My father executed My three elder brothers and not one of us felt safe. I fear God, Pontius, and if this man Jesus will not stay dead, then We have set ourselves against a power most terrible!

Dear Pontius, you are proving such a comfort to Me. I promise I shall not let Tiberius forget it!

HEROD ANTIPAS REX

MILITARY INTELLIGENCE

Report Forma
Classification: SECRET
Copies Only To: H. E. The Governor General, & Director
Military Intelligence.
From: Marcus Sylvanus (Agent LXVI)
Subject: Iesus of Nazareth (Code Name "SALVATOR")
Date: Nonis. Apr.   **Report No.** X/I.C.

I have the honour to submit my preliminary report re.
Bodysnatching and resurrection rumours concerning SALVATOR.

This agent infiltrated the ranks of the Nazarene Party posing as a believing follower, and has kept them under close surveillance for the past six months during which time he has submitted divers reports to Central Intelligence.

I stayed with them during the trial and execution after which they scattered and went into hiding, but I soon traced the inner caucus to one of their familiar hide-outs in the old quarter of the city where I carefully noted their conduct and reactions to the demise of SALVATOR.

The effect of his death upon them was overpowering. All were of the opinion that the 'Messias' could not die, so that the initial impact was to cause complete and utter demoralization. J. Iscariot, for example, our counter-agent (Code name "SQUEALER") has already committed "felo de se" and the Deputy Leader, Simon Peter, was reduced to such a state of abject terror that in my hearing he thrice denied any connection with the proscribed party. At this point the cock crowed and he fled the assembly, threw himself on the ground and wept like a child. The women, particularly Maria, widow of Joseph, and mother of SALVATOR and Maria of Magdala, the ex-cabaret artiste and former mistress of a certain centurion (now posted home) were in a state of profound shock. I mention these examples merely to confirm the success of the execution as a demoralizing force, not only among the inner caucus but with the whole rag tag and bobtail that remains of the party members.

It is this agent's opinion that the whole matter would have ended there, had it not been for the spoliation of the grave and its subsequent effect upon mind and morale. The next of kin were very concerned at being unable to complete the traditional burial honours, owing to the Feast of the Passover. Therefore SALVATOR had been hastily entombed without the customary recital of psalms. Thus the womenfolk decided to make an attempt to perform these funerary rites directly the feast ended. They conferred among themselves as to how they were going to obtain access to the mausoleum which was now sealed and heavily guarded. They decided that in the event of being unable to obtain entry they would festoon the entrance with flowers and conduct the "Psalmae pro Defunctis" outside, or as near to the entrance as they were permitted to approach by the duty guard.

Most of the night was spent discussing the ways and means, for at this point no one made any reference to the possibility of a "resurrection"; as I said previously, they were so utterly demoralized all they could think of was how to complete the correct funerary honours, and the discussion of same seemed to give them some degree of comfort.

I had just dropped off to sleep when I was aroused in the early hours by a commotion. Maria of Magdala and Maria the mother of James, and Joanna Chusa wife of H.M. Herod's Chief Steward were shaking with a mixture of excitement, fear and joy. Everyone was talking at once, but I gathered that these women had set out for the tomb at first light, armed with spices and ointments, only to find the door open, the tomb empty and the duty guard in an unconscious condition. The first reaction by the men was that grave-robbers had stolen the body. Much argument ensued, during which the women, when they had calmed down a little, insisted that this was not the case. They had entered the tomb and seen a young man in a white robe sitting there. Maria of Magdala in her highly excitable condition said his garments were whiter than snow and his face was "like lightning". They had been extremely afraid. But the alleged entity calmed them with words to the effect: "Don't be so surprised. You seek Jesus of Nazareth who was crucified. He is not here for he has risen and is going ahead of you to Galilee."

The other Maria's account differed somewhat. She imagined she had seen not one but two apparitions who said: "Why do you seek the living among the dead? Remember how he told you back in Galilee that he would be crucified and would rise again on the third day!"

I mention this in detail to stress the fact that up till that moment not one of the party had any real hope or belief in a resurrection. To them SALVATOR had failed completely, died miserably, and their whole little dream world had come tumbling down upon their heads. This was confirmed by the extremely sceptical attitude of the men, who told the women they were being stupid and hysterical!

Then Simon Peter said the only way to find out was to go and see for themselves, so despite their fear of being recognized some of them set out at the double for the cemetery, but this agent, still very sceptical decided to wait for them to come back with some more accurate information before going to make a proper inspection and filing his report.

They returned shortly, and confirmed that the tomb had indeed been opened and the body removed, but were still inclined to the opinion that it was the work of grave-robbers. A little later Maria of Magdala returned from a second visit to the tomb, in a state of unusual exaltation. It appeared that in her traumatic condition she had confused the cemetery gardener with SALVATOR. She blabbed out a rather disturbing tale as to how she had stood inside the tomb weeping (she also appeared to think she saw the "two men in white") at which point a man came up behind her, and enquired as to the nature of her grief. She said she replied: "Because they have stolen the body of my Lord and I don't know where they've taken him, and we want to anoint him and sing psalms and pay our last respects. And if it's you who've taken him away, please, sir, tell me where you've put him so we can have his body." The gardener then spoke her name: "Maria!" and she turned round and saw him silhouetted against the tomb entrance. Mistaking him for SALVATOR she hugged him and clung to him (proving he was no ghost!) but he told her not to touch him using words I find difficult to understand (if indeed they were words correctly reported) "Touch me not, for I have not yet ascended to my Father. Go back to my brethren and tell them I am going up to him who is my Father and your Father, who is my God and your God." Apparently it was this strange statement that confirmed her delirious notion that the gardener was in fact her lord resurrected.

I thereupon went myself to the cemetery as quickly as possible. My report thereon is as follows:—

(I) The guards were still unconscious, lying around in an apparently drunken condition. I picked my way through them carefully as I wished to make my examination of the rifled tomb, undisturbed.

(II) The tomb was open as stated, and the stone door had been moved a distance of about fifteen feet. No immediate signs of damage by forcible entry.

(III) The interior was empty of all persons. No sign of any body. But I was surprised by certain factors not usually associated with grave-robbing. Of these, the most curious was the condition of the funeral linen. Instead of being strewn in disarray as would be expected if the body had been hastily unwrapped and removed, it was neatly and correctly folded from top to bottom. The head-piece (or "veil" as the Jews call it) was set apart from the main shroud and was still wound about in the rough shape of the head it had recently contained, making it difficult to see how it could have been removed from the head without unwinding, and also posing the question as to why robbers in a hurry would bother with the almost impossible task of re-winding it without the head inside it to give it form and support.

(IV) On examining the shroud itself, I discovered further inconsistencies. It appears as if the upper part had, without being unwrapped, collapsed suddenly downwards upon the under part to which it had become adhered by reason of congealing blood and other bodily fluids. I inspected it closely a number of times (the sun had now risen and there was excellent light entering the tomb) and I reluctantly came to the conclusion pending further evidence) that neither the veil nor the shroud could not have been unwrapped nor could the body have been withdrawn therefrom by *any known means*.

(V)   It is of course quite impossible that the body should have been "dematerialized" out from its wrappings, so I respectfully suggest the Forensic Dept. takes over and subjects it to a thorough scientific analysis. Meanwhile this agent hastens to reassure his Superiors that, unlike common soldiery he is NOT subject to hallucinations and that when they come to examine the wrappings for themselves they will confirm the difficulties of ascertaining the body's method of exit therefrom.

(VI) Lastly, as a result of the demeanour of the party members, displaying a mixture of shock, disbelief, amazement, stress, it is the considered opinion of this agent that they had no *a priori* knowledge of what was to take place and took no part in the body's removal. The culprits must therefore be sought elsewhere.

But rest assured, I am keeping them under closest surveillance and will report each and every development.

I have the Honour to be, Sir,
Your Most Obt Svt
Special Agent LXVI

CLASSIFICATION	SECRET
FOR OFFICIAL VSE ONLY	PREPARED BY
File! *Q*	*MARCVS SYLVANVS* LXVI

MILITARY INTELLIGENCE

Report Forma
Classification: **SECRET**
Copies Only To: (I) H.E. The Governor General.
  (II) Director, Military Intelligence.
  (III) Central Intelligence, Rome.
  (IV) H.G. The Primate.
From: Marcus Sylvanus (Agent LXVI)
Subject: "SALVATOR" **Report No:** XI/I.C.
Date: a.d. VI Id. Apr.

I have the honour to report that:
Following the failure to date by Military Intelligence, and Temple
Security to locate the body of SALVATOR, and the failure of the
Police and Military Garrison even to provide a passible substitute
I continue my assignment of surveillance maintaining my pose as an
inner-party member (if you could call anything so fragmented and
disorganized a "party").

It remains the opinion of this agent that the party has now
been neutralized and is not of the least danger to the security of the
State. They have barely five hundred members (most of which are
in hiding or have fled to Galilee and other rural areas). The remainder appear quite harmless and might be generally classified as
a mild "lunatic fringe".

Reports, however, continue to come in that A or B has seen or
spoken with the risen SALVATOR, and other reports will doubtless
continue to come in until the whole matter is seen to be nothing
more than a nine-day wonder, by which measure the less attention
we pay to it the quicker that should come about. Needless to say,
not one of these rumours on being investigated has the least scientific
foundation. All they go to demonstrate is the powerful effect
SALVATOR had on their minds and the profound emotional gap left
in their lives by his departure.

I feel reasonably qualified to speak as I was a student of mental
sciences before being drafted, and could quote a number of relevant
cases from the works of my erstwhile tutor, Prof. Carolus Iuvenus
under whom I was studying, but alas my textbooks were left in
Rome when I was posted on foreign service.

Having seen their little dream world shattered, they cling to
any shred of hope, any fantasy, any rumour (or rumour of rumours)

to bolster their shaken confidence. Thus, I am convinced, at this stage, that they are no more than a group of harmless religious maniacs (non-violent, unlike the "Zealots") suffering from shock and profound insecurity. They were all keyed up to see great glory for themselves. Their leader was to become a king greater than Caesar, and the thought of so much power went to their poor little heads – understandable when you consider their drab humdrum existence – fishermen ennobled, tax collectors in highest office, publicans directing the affairs of a pan-celesto-mundane empire: ex-cabaret dancers as 'First Ladies' – who, in their position, could have resisted such blandishments?

Needless to say the rumour first started with the women: with Maria of Magdala the dancer (who adored him) and it was she who first thought she saw him in the person of the Golgotha gardener (suggest Intelligence find the actual gardener and question him). Then Maria, mother of James, and Joanna Chusa thought they had seen him. And thus follows an interesting, almost text-book example of how the collective illusion spreads.

On that same day, Simon Cleophas and another follower were fleeing the city (as have many of his party) and making their way back to Emmaus, a distance of some *sixty furlongs* (I stress this distance deliberately). During the long walk they were joined by (they said) a stranger who asked them what all their excited talk was about? They replied: "Haven't you heard? You must be about the only pilgrim who hasn't heard about Jesus and his trial and crucifixion." The stranger joined them and accompanied them the rest of the way to Emmaus where they asked him to dine with them at the inn. They also told the stranger about the women who'd found the tomb open and then came rushing back saying they'd seen SALVATOR but that none of the men took this seriously, as they'd seen nothing – only an empty tomb. During the walk and during dinner the stranger apparently spoke learnedly, quoting a number of prophecies which would tend to confirm their hopes of resurrection.

As a result, these two hurried back to Jerusalem where they found the rest of the party barricaded in the upper room of James Zebedee's house in the old quarter – barricaded for fear of arrest. No sooner had they got inside than they were entertained to the fantastic story that SALVATOR had been in this upper room a short while before, in the pink of health, and had enjoyed supper with them.

At this point Cleophas (disappointed no doubt at missing him) decided that the stranger at Emmaus was also SALVATOR – something about the way he broke bread seemed familiar. And to convince himself further he said: "Were not our hearts burning when he spoke to us on the road making the scriptures plain to us?" In retrospect he had now determined the stranger looked like SALVATOR after all.

They seemed quite oblivious to one or two minor points –

(a) Why didn't they recognize their master on the road or during dinner? Was he disguised?

(b) How, pray, could any man walk sixty furlongs on recently crucified feet? This man didn't even limp!

(c) Above all how could SALVATOR have dined in Emmaus *and* in Jerusalem almost simultaneously!!!

Really, the whole thing is too ludicrous! And when the women recover their sanity we should hear no more of it. The only sane one in the entire group is Thomas Didymus (a qualified lawyer) whose scornful reaction to the general hysteria was: "Until I have seen the mark of the nails, and put my hand into his side, you will never make me believe!"

I assume the authorities will have found the body and punished the grave-robbers in a matter of days. In anticipation of which I respectfully request that I be relieved of this assignment and returned to normal duties, and (if His Excellency will endorse my petition) that I be posted back to Rome where I sincerely believe I could be of far greater service to His Imperial Majesty.

> I have the Honour to be,
>> Sir,
>>> Your Most Obt Svt
>>>> Special Agent LXVI

CLASSIFICATION	**SECRET**
FOR OFFICIAL VSE ONLY	PREPARED BY
Delete final para before submitting to H.E. *Q*	*MARCVS SYLVANVS* LXVI

MILITARY INTELLIGENCE

OFFICE OF THE DIRECTOR

Classification: CONFIDENTIAL
To: Agent LXVI
From: Director
Subject: "Salvator" Your latest report
Date: a.d. V Id. Apr.

No, Marcus, you may not go home. Most of us have done years in this benighted country. You will do your full span and like it!

Don't you think we aren't all equally homesick, above all H.E. who longs for the cool pines of the Tuscan Hills? But for your sake, dear boy, and because you have shown such promise in the field of counter-intelligence, and to save you from incurring H.E.'s displeasure I have deleted the improperly presented request from your final para. and advise you to restrain yourself from this sort of thing in future. If you wish to be relieved of your duties, complete Resignation Forma A; (but I do not advise it!).

Boring as it is, I genuinely sympathize with you – having to submit your brilliant intellect to the uninspiring company of these Jewish peasants which must be most tedious, but you are doing a most necessary job, and your reports must continue until the missing body has been located and publicly exposed. So you will carry on with your assignment exactly as directed. Or would you prefer a nice long desert march with C. and E. Cohorts who leave tomorrow for the Egyptian frontier?

Not too much speculation please. Just facts!

Q.
Director of Military Intelligence

PP

a.d. V. Kal. Apr.

My Dear Caiaphas,

As you are doubtless well aware, Military Intelligence have to date failed to apprehend the grave robbers or – worse – to discover the whereabouts of the remains of Jesus of Nazareth. Nor, I gather, have your own agents proved any more successful.

Meanwhile, rumours and counter-rumours of his alleged resurrection continue to multiply and spread like a swarm of locusts. So that I fear that unless we recover the body very shortly there is the strong possibility that the lunatic fringe could set off another wave of extremism, leading to further riots and unrest which, I am *sure* you will appreciate, could be at least as damaging to you as it could be to me. Thus, if we cannot find his actual body, it may prove necessary to "arrange" one. Should you have in your tender care any prisoner approaching his fine physique and appearance please let me know at once. A little intelligent mutilation could disguise many small dissimilarities. I fear the wretches awaiting death in our salubrious cells consist entirely (at the moment) of half-starved thieves and scrofulous recidivists who would make very poor substitutes.

I have never particularly liked you, nor have your recent actions further endeared you to me. To add to my troubles, the Lady Claudia has refused to speak to me since the execution, and it is quite impossible to make her understand the unpleasant necessities of political expediency – women do not share your cold, reasoned logic. But as we are now both in this – up to our necks – I suggest we cease quarrelling and combine forces.

BURN AFTER READING.

Yours,

PONTIVS

PALACE OF
THE PRIMATE

a.d. IV Kal. Apr.

My Dear Governor General,

Or, may I take the liberty of calling you "Pontius"?? It does my heart good that we can let bygones be bygones, united at last, so it seems, by common weal and woe.

Far be if from me to contradict you, but I cannot for the very life of me imagine who's been putting ideas in Your Excellency's head concerning my true and innermost feelings for you which, I swear by all the Gold in the Temple, have ever been of the highest admiration, respect and affection. Even were I not commanded by Holy Charity to love all mankind equally as myself, my sincerest affection for you would in no wise be diminished.

But coming to the pressing matter in hand, I too regret that I have no prisoner whose body might possibly be substituted for that of the Traitor; and its public exhibition – however disfigured – would soon be recognized as a deceit and would only make matters worse. Therefore I think we should allow our very efficient Intelligence Services a little more time to locate the original. But, if "resurrection" rumours continue to persist, I might profitably issue a Pastoral Letter (to be read in all Synagogues) making the wilful spreading of this false and impious rumour a "Reserved Mortal Sin".

This, I can assure you, would produce the desired disciplinary effect!

Oh, but I am sorely grieved to learn of your marital difficulties for which I fear I am partially responsible. Alas, if only Her Excellency were of Our Faith, a Rabbi skilled in marriage-guidance could be provided to convince her of the error (innocent, but nevertheless, error) of her present unfortunate attitude, which I earnestly hope and pray will be short-lived.

I shall, if I may, offer Holy Sacrifice for your Intentions, and most particularly that this temporary rift between you may rapidly be healed.

In the meantime, be good enough to keep me closely informed of every least development so that we may, as you so rightly put it, combine forces to ensure a speedy and successful suppression of these dangerous rumours.

Assuring you of my fullest co-operation.
Yours in Very True Friendship,
CAIAPHAS

Report Forma
Classification: MOST SECRET
Copies Only To: (I)   H.E. The Governor General.
　　　　　　　(II)　Director, Military Intelligence.
　　　　　　　(III) Central Intelligence, Rome.
　　　　　　　(IV) H.G. The Primate.
　　　　　　　(V)　H.M. King Herod

See endorsement Q.

From: Marcus Sylvanus (Agent LXVI)
Subject: SALVATOR　　**Report No:** XII/I.C.
Date: Idibus Apr.

I have the honour to report that:
In compliance with your orders as of last week I remained in close touch with the party. Though most its members have dispersed, the inner caucus still appears to remain intact.

On Monday (yesterday) we were again at James Zebedee's house. We had gone there individually so as not to attract attention and, after we all had entered the upper room, the door (the *only* door, mark you) was firmly locked and bolted. Prayers were said, and at this stage no drinks nor refreshments other than a supper of broiled fish had been served. I wish to stress that point *No intoxicating beverages had been served.* After supper a curious sensation filled the room which I do not know quite how to describe — a tension, an electric feeling as before a thunderstorm, or like the suppressed excitement when the trumpeters come out to herald the chariot race. But yet again – different! Suddenly, all eyes turned, not towards the door, but to the end wall where a figure was standing, to all intents and appearances the image of "Salvator". The effect on the gathering was remarkable – as if they were seeing a ghost. In fact several cried out that it was a phantom.

But it was no phantom. The figure advanced into the light and for a moment I was tempted to share the general belief that it was none other than "Salvator" in the flesh. He came forward smiling, which was strange, for the wounds of recent execution were most apparent. Even though he appeared the double of "Salvator" there was an imperceptible difference – thinner perhaps, a slight change in personality; I don't know. My eyes told me it was him. But some inner sense told me it was not.

I was about to risk my life by apprehending him when he called out: "Peace be upon you!" Then, turning to Thomas Didymus he took his hand saying: "Give me your finger. See, here are my hands." Nervously, Thomas felt the nail wounds without appearing to cause any pain. Then he said: "Let me have your hand, put it in my side." And Thomas reluctantly thrust his hand deep into what appeared to be a spear wound on the right side of the body, again without appearing to cause any discomfiture. I noticed, too, that the wounds, though recent, were clean and free from suppuration.

Then the newcomer smiled at him: "Stop all this doubting, Thomas! Believe!" And Thomas fell down on his knees crying: "My Lord and my God!"

The figure answered: "Because you have seen me and touched me you have believed. But happy are those who have not seen and yet learned to believe!" Then to top it all he suddenly turned and demanded: "I'm hungry. What's for supper?"

Having partially recovered from their shock they managed to scrape up some sort of a meal which the newcomer ate avidly. He appeared to be enjoying himself immensely as would one reunited with his old friends. During which I seized this opportunity to make a quick examination of the room. The door was still firmly locked and bolted and the window-shutters had not been disturbed. The diners were so preoccupied that I was able to examine the walls and floor without attracting notice. But on this cursory investigation I could not detect any crack or cavity that would lend a clue to the cunningly contrived secret passage by which this clever conjurer could only have entered. (I recommend a thorough search and investigation at a suitable time.)

Purely from a social viewpoint the dinner was an unqualified success. The menu though simple was amply compensated by the unbounded joy of the participants at finding what they truly imagined to be their old friend and leader back from the dead, and with a healthy man's appetite (presumably rations are short in Hades for he ate like a man who hadn't had a square meal in days!). At least this ruled out any possibility that it was a ghost. The "Records of the Imperial Society for Psychic Research" instance numbers of cases of full materialization, but always through the agency of a Sybil or deep trance medium (there was no one present asleep or entranced at the time); and always in darkness or in faint red light (correct me if I am wrong) and never lasting more than a few minutes at a time.

(i)   There was no medium I could discern.

(ii) The room was lit by oil lamps (yellow/white light)

(iii) The manifestation persisted well over an hour.

We can therefore exclude all probability of psychic phenomenon.

The second theory to explore is that it was indeed the person of 'Salvator', revived from deep swoon (Jove knows by what black arts) though how any one, even of his fine physique, could ever survive crucifixion and a spear-thrust through the heart on the heels of a severe flogging is quite beyond me. Though it is understandable that the duty guard may have been drugged, it remains yet to explain how the tomb could have been opened from inside (as lack of tool-marks show was the case) by a man in his weakened condition who had suffered catatonic trance.

The third, and more likely, theory, is that he has a double, or twin brother, capable of deceiving even his closest followers. However, I continued to observe the subject, taking a firm hold of my senses and determined to ascertain how he would make his exit (assuming the method to be the same as of entry). At one time he looked up from the table, giving me the uncomfortable sensation that he was reading my thoughts. My discomfiture increased when he gently shook his head and appeared as if he were about to laugh at me, making me feel about one cubit high. Feeling in need of a drink I arose and went to the wine jars. As I was filling my glass there was a very faint sound like a silent cold rush of air and I felt 'goosepimples' rising on my spine. I swung round, but too late. He had vanished – disappeared the way he had come.

SUMMARY
(I)   Psychic phenomena of a very high order.
        EVALUATION Negative. (as per the above)
(II)   "Salvator" himself, recovered.
        EVALUATION. Most unlikely. No man could survive what
        he underwent. Even had he, by some miracle survived, he
        would be in no state to sit there enjoying dinner and chatting
        to his friends.
(III)   If (II) is to be accepted then the Execution Squad should be
        courtmartialled for dereliction in the line of duty and/or
        Conspiracy to obstruct the course of justice.
(IV)   A Twin or double. Suggest careful scrutiny: 'Registrar of
        Births and Deaths' Bethlehem Urban District.
(V)   In conjunction with (IV) a cunningly contrived secret
        entrance. Request search at earliest opportunity.

EVALUATION
    The only possible solutions are IV and V. The above recom-
mended action should shortly confirm this.

                    I have the Honour to be,
                        Sir,
                        Your Obt Svt
                                Special Agent LXVI

CLASSIFICATION	TOP SECRET
FOR OFFICIAL VSE ONLY	PREPARED BY
Copies not, repeat NOT to come any-where near (I) (IV) (V). Particularly (V). Q	*MARCVS SYLVANVS* LXVI

Classification: CONFIDENTIAL
To: Agent LXVI
From: Director
Subject: SALVATOR Your Report No. XII/I.C.
Date: a.d. XVI Kal. Apr.

Marcus, dear boy, your report reads like something between a hag's mag and cheap sci. fi. Far be it for me to doubt the abilities of one of our most lynx-eyed and razor-witted officers, but you must admit your effort makes very poor reading so that I am very dubious of filing it, let alone allowing it to go any higher.

Moreover, your report is confused, badly composed, and tending to suggest that our agent too was not exactly unaffected by the emotive impact which you say was shared by all persons present. However, we have followed your suggestion and made a careful check of the premises. Nothing out of the ordinary was found. Nor, frankly, did we expect to find anything. There was no method of operating the door bolts from the exterior, nor have floor, walls or ceiling been tampered with in any way.

Dear boy, don't you think you may be barking up the wrong tree? If you re-read your own report XI/I.C. carefully you will find the key staring you in the face. Let me quote your own words: "I was aroused in the early morning by a commotion. Maria of Magdala and Maria the mother of James, and *Joanna Chuza, wife of H.M. King Herod's Chief Steward* were shaking with a mixture of excitement, fear and joy."

In the good Mrs Chuza may lie the key to what followed. You see, you tend to underrate the wiles of these "peasants" as you call them. Are you quite sure they don't suspect your identity? Suppose you are already a "blown agent" what could now be more subtly advantageous to their cause than to build upon the women's initial illusion, staging the whole subsequent performance at Zebedee's house for your express benefit? Mrs Chuza has already told her husband who has (unfortunately) told H.M. King Herod; who is quaking in his sandals. This, they know will be backed up by just the kind of report you have written, so that the rumour that Jesus

lives will circulate, not only in royal circles, but will now be sub-
stantiated by Intelligence reports, thereby lending it an aura of
highest credence and respectability.

Herod is superstitious enough, but I dread to think what will
happen if this reaches Her Excellency, with her dreams and 'visions'.
In no time the whole Garrison will be 'seeing him'. Subalterns seeking
advancement will soon find an encounter with the 'risen messias' the
shortest route to promotion. You know what Her Excellency is when
she gets the spiritual bug!

No, Marcus, I think you have very much under-rated your
opponents. They will continue to stage these performances until they
think your reports have done their work and they can come into the
open as the officially sponsored champions of the resurrected prophet.
What a splendid time they will have. With Herod and H.E. now on
their side, they may even be able to insist on SALVATOR being "re-
habilitated" and those responsible for his death severely punished
(which, in a long shot, might even include you and I!)

So I shall tell you what you must do. Continue to play their
game. Pretend you are completely taken in. Let them not suspect
by so much as a wink that you are suspicious. Send in reports when
you can (but don't be caught writing them!) and I shall prevent
these reaching Herod, or Her Excellency until the real body is
found and identified.

Watch carefully, and bide your opportunity to seize and arrest
the imposter. Oh yes, I realize the dangers when you are one among
many. But you are trained to take care of yourself. My guess is there
will soon be a repeat performance. So the more susceptible you
appear, the better. Get them off guard. Try to persuade the imposter
to be alone with you, or to come out of doors – on the road to
Emmaus, for example. Then you can apprehend him or, better, let
him swiftly suffer a 'second death' at the point of your good Roman
sword!

Oh, the beauty of it! Then we shall have our body (whether
that of SALVATOR or his double matters little). So, dead or alive, get
the body to the Praetorium for public viewing and an end to the
whole ridiculous sedition. I can promise you success will merit you
a 'gong', and I'm sure Herod and His Grace of Israel will be more
than appreciative!

Q.

Director, Military Intelllgence.

MILITARY INTELLIGENCE

Report Forma
Classification MOST SECRET

"EYES ONLY DIRECTOR MILITARY INTELLIGENCE"

From: Agent LXVI
Subject: SALVATOR
Date: a.d. VII Kal. Apr.   **Report No.** XIII/I.C.

Sir,

I have the honour to report that I have read your Memo and advice most carefully, and must confess that the possibilities you put forward had not entered my mind. But with respect I should like to point out that the cunning with which you attribute these simple people seems out of all proportion to their intellectual abilities. To have staged for my benefit the episode related in Report No. XII/I.C. would require tremendous rehearsal and team-work. I admit that reports reaching King Herod via Mrs Chuza might have encouraged them, but would not the same hold good if we re-considered the "swoon theory", and assumed the seismic subsidence caused the tomb to open, enabling the followers to take him away and revive him?

Having decided he was going to live, they could have started putting about resurrection rumours, even providing a "double" until such time as the real SALVATOR is fit and well to take his rightful place walking about (wound-scars and all) as the first Prophet to come back from the "dead". If this be the case, it is just possible they may have been capable of fabricating the incident at the house of James Zebedee, and that the acting was not as good as I imagined, but only appeared marvellous under the supercharged emotional conditions (which perhaps I suffered more than the others!) We can obviously discount the Emmaus "appearance" as wishful-thinking-after-the-event.

You know what this country is? Dervishes, prophets, wild men of the desert, conjurers, wonder-workers, unidentified celestial objects (read Ezekiel I to VII) pillars of fire, burning bushes, ladders with a brisk two-way traffic in angels? The whole damn country is half mad. The sun and the desert do strange things to men's minds. Oh give me good old down-to-earth (and to bed) gods of Noble Rome. You know where you are with Jupiter and his dams. Life, good lusty Roman life! None of your invisible Jehovah nonsense! I fear if we stay here too long we shall all be in danger of succumbing. They say the old legionnaires who settle here become more Jewish than the Jews. That I have seen and believed.

But back to your original theory, Sir, I am bound to admit that even for a man of his physique to be walking around three days after an unsuccessful crucifixion does take considerable explaining. It should be months, maybe years before he could stagger from his hospital bed (in whatever secret cave that may be) and I saw him wolf down a meal to satisfy a cohort. So whether SALVATOR himself be dead or alive, I fully agree that the man I saw must be a double, whose real identity may be known only to an inner few. The fewer the better, for it would make the reactions of the uninitiated completely genuine, and therefore very convincing to a slightly bewildered (at the time) Roman Agent.

Rest assured, I shall apprehend him on his next appearance, to which I am looking forward with some relish.

I have the Honour to be,

Sir,

Your Obt Svt

Special Agent LXVI

CLASSIFICATION	**TOP SECRET**
FOR OFFICIAL VSE ONLY	PREPARED BY
Check out Registrar Births, Deaths and Marriages (Bethlehem) for possible twin. *Q* *Registry check – Negative.* *P.L.C.*	*MARCVS SYLVANVS* LXVI

MILITARY INTELLIGENCE
MEMORANDVM FORMA

To: Agent LXVI
From: Director.
Date: a.d. V Kal. Apr.

A body. Just get us a body! That is all!

pp Director, (O.C. i/c) Intelligence.

MILITARY INTELLIGENCE

Report Forma
Classification: **MOST SECRET**
Copy Only To: DIRECTOR INTELLIGENCE
From: Agent LXVI
Subject: SALVATOR   Report Number XIV/I.C.
Date: Pridie Nonas Maias

Sir,

I have the honour to report that I regret the difficulties of keeping you appraised of the situation during the past two weeks, but I had decided that my only chance of apprehending SALVATOR (or his double) was to keep the inner caucus under close observation, which meant I had to go with them to Galilee, where they have reverted to their normal occupations. As a result I have spent many horrible hours as a "fisherman" on the Sea of Tiberias suffering from acute seasickness – to which I am more than prone!

There had been no further manifestations of SALVATOR since my last report (XII/I.C.) and I was beginning to lose heart, suspecting that they were now aware of my true identity, and had decided to act very cautiously until I tired of my vigil and departed. Night after night I've been out in their beastly little boats (you know the storms that whip that lake into sudden fury) and last night I felt I could endure it no longer. I really felt I must have one good night's sleep and leave them to their own devices. To be frank I had determined to halt a courier on the morrow and send you a report stating they had tired of their masquerades, resumed their former occupations, and that (as I originally prophesied) the whole business was nothing more than a nine day wonder.

This morning, however, an event took place which shows that, regardless of whether they suspect my identity, the SALVATOR plot is far from finished. After yesterday's gale, I felt I could not face the Sea again, so I opted out of the night's fishing and slept in a copse near the shore. I awoke this morning to the delicious smell of a really good fish-fry. I saw smoke blowing towards me from about two hundred yards down the beach where all the boats had pulled in and their crews gathered round a fire. Hungry for breakfast I made my way along the shore and, as I approached, a person looking uncommonly like SALVATOR detached himself from the group and looked in my direction. The whole group were now watching me, making me feel very conspicuous. I was mentally weighing up the odds, wondering whether I could effect an arrest against such numbers when the SALVATOR (or his double) seemed to vanish into thin air.

I ran forward to be greeted with merriment. They told me I had not only just missed SALVATOR, but also missed seeing them make the biggest catch ever recorded. There were about a hundred and fifty (CL) huge fat fish, less those already charcoal-grilled and eaten for breakfast. Everyone was in exceptionally good spirits and kept sympathizing with me on missing their experience – which irked me as I hate to feel I've been outwitted.

Apparently they'd spent a completely fruitless night, trawling the Sea until dawn, when they decided to give it up as a bad job. They said *a man* had been waiting for them on the shore who is alleged to have called out: "Friends, have you caught anything?" They had told him in their fisherman's vernacular what they thought of the lake and its fishing. But apparently this man persuaded them to try again, saying that if they cast their nets from the starboard side of the boat they'd do much better. They did as told, and before they were more than a few hundred yards from the shore the nets were filled to breaking-point – so heavy they could not wind them in but had to tow them ashore. *Only at this point did the disciple John decide the stranger was* SALVATOR. He shouted: "It's the Lord!" whereupon, Simon Peter, impetuous as ever, leapt into the water and waded ashore followed by many others. Meanwhile it seems SALVATOR had got a charcoal fire going, and he calmly greeted them with the invitation: "Come and have breakfast." So they all enjoyed a fish barbecue with him, during which he told them to preach his message to all the nations of the world. He also told them a number of other things which they declined to divulge to me. When I joined them they were all in extremely good spirits such as any fisherman would be after a record catch. But when I listened to their tale, certain parts of it struck me as very odd.

If once more they had concocted it for my benefit, why did they pretend they did not recognize the newcomer as SALVATOR until *after* they had made their catch? They also said that, despite John and Peter recognizing him, not one of them dared ask his identity, even while sitting with him sharing their breakfast. All this seems most inconsistent with a fabrication! Surely it would have sounded more convincing to me if they'd told me they recognized him from the first moment they saw him waiting on the beach; or at least, at the moment he spoke, asking if they'd had any luck with their catch?

I confess I am becoming more and more confused. There are too many discrepancies to account properly either for a conspiracy, or a genuine return from the dead. But, as ordered, I shall continue my surveillance and file reports whenever possible.

I have the Honour to be,
Sir,
Your Obt Svt
Agent LXVI

CLASSIFICATION	**TOP SECRET**
FOR OFFICIAL VSE ONLY	PREPARED BY
Disciplinary action? *P.L.C.* *NO! (not yet!)* Q	*MARCVS SYLVANVS* LXVI

MILITARY INTELLIGENCE
OFFICE OF THE DIRECTOR

Classification: CONFIDENTIAL
To: Agent LXVI
From: Director
Subject: SALVATOR Your Report No. XIV/I.C.
Date: Nonis Mai

Marcus, dear boy,

This is your third failure. Not only have you failed to locate the body, nor attempted to elucidate its place of concealment from party members, but you have had at least three occasions on which an opportunity presented itself to apprehend the impersonator, but either through fear or lack of initiative, failed to do so!

The Department is fully aware that you have at all times been outnumbered, but you have your small-arms and your self-defence kit concealed about your person. You inform us that party members are unarmed, so we can see no viable reason why you should not have displayed a little more courage and personal initiative.

It is the Order of the Department that on his next "manifestation" you shall reveal yourself, produce your Imperial Warrant and demand the imposter surrenders himself quietly. At the sight of Caesar's Seal, no Jew would dare assault you. Even if they should be so ill advised, your costly post-gladiatoral course was not given for your amusement and it should make you more than a match for a group of barbarians.

We expect positive results from you at very next opportunity or you will be relieved of your assignment and explain yourself to less tolerant Authority than –

Q.
Director, Military Intelligence

FORMA 'A' (RESIGNATION)

Date *a.d. VII Id. Iun*

Sir,
I wish to submit my resignation (in triplicate) from the Service. I regret I am no longer able to fulfil the duties allotted to me. I wish to reassure my Superiors of my continued unswerving loyalty to Caesar and to the Oath I took under the Official Secret's Act. Nothing of what I have done nor witnessed will ever be divulged to a living soul other than when ordered by Proper Authority. I humbly request that I be returned to General Duties, and fully realize that I shall forfeit my present rank and the privileges and promotion normal to the Special Service.

> I have the Honour to be
> Sir
> Your Ob Svt
> *MARCVS SYLVANVS*
> Agent LXVI

WRITE CLEARLY AND ON BOTH SIDES

IF ANYTHING IS ENCLOSED THIS LETTER WILL BE DESTROYED

To: DIRECTOR, MILITARY INTELLIGENCE
From: M. Sylvanus, (Former Captain, Special Service)
Date: (a.d. XII Kal. Oct. DCCLXXVIII)

Sir,

I have spent many years in The Service and, as you know, have always done my utmost to serve Caesar and my lawful Superiors. My Reports have ever been as accurate and truthful as is humanly possible, and have on more than one occasion played no small part in preventing bloodshed and disorders before such events could mature. You also know that during the many happy years I served under your Command, never once have I altered so much as a single word of any such report made by me, neither to please a superior nor even to avoid embarrassment in high places, if what I had already set out was true to my best knowledge and belief.

It is therefore particularly distressing to me that you should now feel that I have failed you in my most recent (and as it happens, final) mission, ending my life in disgrace; a discredit to The Service in which you take such especial pride; or that I may seem to have betrayed one who befriended me as a junior officer, teaching me every trick and nuance of our art – you to whom I owe any skill I might ever have acquired.

I am not pleading for mercy. Please don't think that for one instant. I accept my fate, whatever it may be. Indeed compared to that meted out to non-citizens, the punishment dealt to me, a Roman, will be relatively swift, at which I trust and pray I shall bear myself with fitting dignity and courage. I am not complaining. Nor am I asking you to intercede at this last minute on my behalf. For seen through official eyes I must have most lamentably failed in my Duty; and my Sentence is correct and just. But it is how I may now appear through *your* eyes, the eyes of my most respected Superior Officer and – dare I say it? – old friend that distresses me beyond bearing. So I am therefore taking it upon myself to relate to you, honestly, accurately and without any exaggeration, the amazing events that led up to and forced (I had no choice) my resignation and present incarceration.

Following your last instructions, I once more re-examined the whole case, probing, analysing, exploring every possibility; seeking for any little piece of evidence (however apparently small or unimportant) that might hitherto have been overlooked and which might throw any new light on this most baffling case. During my assignment as an infiltrator I had seen and heard Salvator many times prior to his trial and execution so that I was utterly convinced I should recognize him anywhere, under any circumstances, or guise. For he was (is) a man of singular appearance and physique. So I must confess that when I first saw him again after his death (or what then appeared to be him) I was caused almost as much mental shock and confusion as it caused his followers. Now, in my several previous reports we explored a series of possibilities to account for his apparent reanimation, of which the most likely two were either that he had made a miraculous recovery and returned to normal health in a matter of hours (which we ruled out as impossible) or else that he was being impersonated by a double, mainly for my benefit so as to confuse Intelligence; and for the purpose of a most elaborate and tortuous political plot – neither of which as it so happens are correct – and for a while you were inclined to favour the second of these theories. But at my final encounter when I saw him face to face in broad daylight I was forced into the most uncomfortable conclusions that the man I saw was either Jesus himself, or an absolutely identical twin.

Registrar of Births, Deaths and Marriages (Bethlehem District) confirm that Maria his mother gave birth only to a single son some thirty-three years ago. On being discreetly questioned, none of his immediate relatives or disciples revealed any knowledge of a twin brother. Nor had Jesus, who had often spoken of his relatives in my hearing, ever so much as hinted at one. Certainly there is quite a strong family resemblance among his relatives; particularly James. But no one could possibly mistake James for him, or vice versa; least of all the followers and party members who were every bit as confused initially as was your humble servant.

Even so, I still had not completely ruled out the possibility of a double until recent events proved to me beyond every shadow of a doubt that if a double did exist then he too was possessed of the same supra-normal powers as Jesus himself. On the very last occasion he shared a meal with us he told us not to leave the City but to remain there and witness "the fulfilment of the Father's promise". And he added for emphasis: "You have heard it from my own lips." Then he went on to say that whereas John (beheaded by Herod) was baptized only by water, we were to receive a much greater form of baptism very shortly. I quote his words: "a baptism by the Holy Spirit". Of course, at that time, none of us had the slightest idea what he meant, and the more politically minded questioned him at length. For they were still under the impression that he was about to restore Israel to Jewish rule, possibly with a great show of celestial force against which even our mighty legions could do nothing. "Do you mean you are going to restore dominion to Israel here and now?" they asked. But he shook his head, seeing they still, despite all his teaching, had little understanding of who and what he was. "It's not for you to know the times and seasons which the Father has fixed by his own authority" he answered. "It's quite enough for you to know that the Holy Spirit will come upon you, and you will receive great strength from it. And you are to be my witnesses in Jerusalem and throughout Judaea, in Samaria, yes, even to the very ends of the Earth." Whereupon he rose and announced we should all set out for Bethany. It struck me that here at last was the opportunity I had been waiting for to apprehend him. I would wait till we were on the open road where I would endeavour to separate him from his companions and arrest him without difficulty. Or, if we remained in a group, we would have every chance of passing a company of police or soldiers whom I could immediately summon to my assistance. I felt jubilant. At last, my good fellow, I've got you – so I thought as I accompanied them quietly, waiting, watching, just biding my time. I felt the exaltation of a hunter nearing the end of the chase. At last my curiosity would be gratified. The mystery would be solved. And I – oh I could see it – would come in for the highest praise and commendation. But as we left the City a strange uneasiness overtook me I felt less confident. I had nagging doubts; was I betraying him?

On the road he spoke of many things which I did not understand. But merely to listen to the captivating modulations of his voice not only convinced me that he was Jesus, but filled me with a remarkable sense of well-being, calm and happiness. All thoughts of arresting or harming him seemed to leave my mind. Just as on the first balmy days of spring you completely forget you have ever shivered in the cold. Then as we reached the summit of Mount Olivet he halted, meditated for a few minutes in silence; then turned and blessed us.

His face had become luminous, whether from reflections of the light that was now increasing all around us, or luminous from within, I cannot be sure. But I did notice the faces of his companions appeared no different. The sky had suddenly become very bright, not like normal sunlight but a vivid kind of diffused radiance that seemed to be emanating from an almost circular cloud that had appeared overhead. The light increased and it became difficult to look without squinting at the dazzling whiteness (increasing every minute now) that surrounded him, was all about him, and was of him. He spoke strangely – that he had to leave us to go to other sheep in other folds. He spoke of the plurality of worlds; that in his Father's house there were many mansions. But that were he was going we could not follow him. From time to time he looked upwards with an expression of indescribable happiness. Already he seemed to be seeing with some inner vision a multiplicity of worlds and heaven-worlds; worlds without end, to which he was very shortly to go, and to which – for obvious reasons – we could not yet accompany him.

Then slowly he raised his arms and looked at us for the last time. We were many, yet he seemed to be looking directly at each one of us. He looked into my eyes and I saw something I shall never forget to my dying day – the ultimate bliss of a being united in body, in spirit and in consciousness with the Supreme Power, that Power we comprehend dimly under so many names; different in every tribe, creed and country. The light increased and the air seemed to crackle. I sensed then – though my physical ears did not hear it – a wondrous musical chord, an harmonic such as the Music of the Spheres, the Tonic Note of all the heavens. The lights separated into a thousand radiant spectra. Glorious colours throbbed and ebbed. Great waves of light seemed to emanate from his heart and from a point in his forehead. And then, slowly at first, almost imperceptibly, he became weightless and began to rise in the air. Time stood still as we watched him, born upward in an indescribable synthesis of beauty. The sound became the light. And all the radiant colours of the light (colours such as I have never seen before) became the sound. It was as if a window in the heavens had opened allowing us a brief, brief, all too brief glimpse into Paradise.

Then, after what may have been minutes, hours or even days – for time seemed to have ceased completely – he entered the very centre of that luminous cloud, and we saw him no longer. As he entered, the cloud began to pulse with ever increasing energy and radiance, sending out dazzling rainbow hues and swiftly changing spectra. Then, the cloud too rose swiftly in the air until it vanished, bearing him away – away to something impossible to describe. I only know, Sir, that if every joy and happiness I have ever known during my span on earth were added together, their total sum would fall far short of those few glorious moments granted me on the summit of Mount Olivet.

While we were still gazing skywards, dazed and straining for just one final sight of him we became aware that two strangers had joined us. They were dressed entirely in white and seemed to have something of his "atmosphere" about them. I do not know who or what they were; where they came from or where they went. They just suddenly appeared. "Men of Galilee," they said. "Why do you stand here gazing heavenwards? He who has just been taken up into heaven – this same Jesus – will return in the same manner as you have just seen him go." Then they too vanished.

Well, in a stunned silence we staggered down the hill back into Jerusalem. Not until we had got indoors and recovered part of our senses were we able to speak and exchange notes of our experience. We could still scarcely credit what we had seen and we made each man relate his tale separately so as to be sure we had all seen and heard the same things. There was no doubt about it. Apart from small personal variations, each man present had enjoyed an identical experience.

I offer no explanation, other than the obvious (the impossible one) that he was truly a Manifestation of the Supreme Cosmic Power, and that this final act triumphantly vindicated each and every promise and earlier marvels. By way of confirmation, Peter held forth at some length quoting relevant passages of their scriptures, and drawing our attention to numerous prophecies which certainly seem to have been amply fulfilled.

I do now most solemnly swear that the above is a true and accurate account of the facts as witnessed by me and by those who were also with me; and that these facts left me with no other choice in conscience other than to resign my commission and reveal myself to those it has been my duty to keep under surveillence. I furthermore freely admit that I broke secrecy, confessed myself before them and begged their forgiveness. They were little moved, for they had long known my true identity. The risen Lord had always known me, but because he makes no distinction between one man and another, regardless of rank, class or creed, had allowed me to remain with them so that I too might be privileged to witness what I had witnessed, and thereby be given the wonderful opportunity (which I did not deserve) of changing my entire way of living and thinking.

It means, of course, that I have utterly failed in my duty to my Emperor. But emperors like all men will die. The King I have seen with my own eyes can now never die, and one day in some far off time and age – I do not agree with their immediate optimism – the whole world and everyone in it will benefit to their profound and everlasting joy.

Now that I had been relieved of the necessity of deceit (and it was a relief indescribable!) I became their friend and confidant. They have become very dear to me. Never once did they rebuke me for my deceit but gave thanks to God that He allowed me to become as one of them and to be baptized. Yes, Sir, again I have to admit that I have been formally initiated into their bond and have accepted their spiritual authority. What else could I do? How I wish you could have been there too! There is nothing greater I could want for one so dear to me.

It was at this point that I sent in my resignation so that I could remain with my new-found friends as long as possible, waiting to see what great events would follow. We did not have long to wait. Doubtless you have already heard the story from others – how the disciples have been rousing the whole City by their eloquent addresses which every man who listens hears in his own native tongue? The effect on these cosmopolitan crowds is unbelievable. Here are Jews, Parthians, Medes, Elamites, Asians, Libyan, Cretans, Egyptians, Arabs, and Romans like ourselves, each hearing the glad tidings being proclaimed in the language of his mother country. These men who had been able to address me only in

197

Hebrew or Aramaic, now gave forth in Patrician Latin without trace of an accent. Yet, a few days earlier they could barely read a Roman street sign, let alone pronounce it properly. I shall reveal to you how all this came about.

We were gathered together in prayer and brotherhood when the room began to tremble. Earthquake! we thought and were frightened. There came a rushing roaring sound like a hurricane. It tore through the house with the speed of a desert whirlwind and for one terrifying moment I thought it was going to be blown off its foundations and we should all perish. But strange to relate, there was no actual movement of the air. Nothing was disturbed; not even the door-curtain stirred. The Power was within the four walls. Then the room filled with a blinding light which separated into the form of cold bright flames that settled on the heads of those happy ones. Cosmic power seemed to flow into their very being, their hearts, their minds, and into their understanding. – in particular their understanding – for when the light departed they were different men. Something in their minds had been opened and for the first time they had glimpsed universal Reality. They had been truly initiated into the knowledge of the Mysteries and the Truth which all men seek. From this moment onwards they were no longer ordinary men like ourselves; confused, brash, throwing our weight about, airing our paltry opinions as if they had some merit. They had transcended the petty limitations of their former personalities which had now merged into a much greater personality – what do we call that Greater Personality – God? I don't know. All I do know is that because of my former activities I was not privileged to share in their sublime experience, but only to be witness to it (for which I am profoundly grateful) as I deserved nothing from the Master I would have tried to betray.

I have no explanation I could possibly offer you. I merely relate the facts to the best of my ability, and this for one reason. I beg you (without causing trouble to yourself or without committing any least action contrary to Caesar, our gracious Emperor) that you will use your good offices to give some measure of protection to these men, the true servants of all that is good and wonderful. It is my earnest prayer that should they fall into your hands during the course of your duties, you will not harm them, for in so doing you could do far greater harm to yourself and even to Rome. Is it perhaps beyond my wildest presumption to hope that you too may take comfort and joy from what they have to tell you and me and anyone who cares to listen?

You see, Sir, these good fellows are not in the least political. What they have to say concerns not just us, nor just Rome, but the whole of mankind. Their glad tidings do not lay down the law, nor set at naught the laws and the justice of our great Roman Civilization. They are merely making you an offer: Would you like to live a new way? Would you like to rid yourself of that dreadful guilt and confusion that haunts mankind and drives him to do things of which he is ashamed? Would you like to enjoy every moment of your life? Would you like to know an inner harmony and peace that no words can describe? That is all they are trying to say to you, to me and to everyone. They are saying: "There aren't any nations. Only people. The world consists only of human beings just waiting to be swep up into that all-kindness we call God."

We have just been given a reprieve from the dreary boring mediocrity of everyday life; and a chance to break down the fears and petty constrictions that bind us. What a wonderful chance is being offered! But I am afraid – I am afraid that those who hear it may not understand and may let it pass them by, leaving them with the empty formalism of dogmatic religion, its narrowness, its self-importance, and its lack of love. If this should be, then let our glorious Cohorts carry the message. For Rome is built not only on power but also on justice; upon the great ideal of a united world where all may come to share the benefits of one single humanity. Sensing this, our philosophers and law-makers have ever been groping towards a mankind united – not by fear – but by desire. Here is the great chance. Take it! Take it! *I beg you, take it!*

As for myself, my little unimportant ex-self. What happens to that is of least importance. Do with it what you have to do. I understand. I have nothing to forgive you. Only, forgive me in your heart wherever I have failed you.

I greet you Dearest "Q" not with "Farewell" but with: "Hail to the Morrow!"

I remain Sir,

Always your most faithful and devoted servant and friend

MARCVS SYLVANVS

(Former Capt. Special Services.)

METEOROLOGICAL OFFICE

CÆSAREA

Date. a.d. III Id. Iun. A.U.C. DCCLXXXVI
REPORT, Ref/ *Peculiar Luminescent Cloud-condensation*

Subsequent to numerous but uncorrelated reports ensuant upon the formation of unusually luminescent cloud-condensation in the regional area in and around that of the Mount of Olives, Idibus Mai, it is the considered opinion of this Department that the said increase in luminosity, spectra-differentiation (rainbow) and scintillation were in every probability occasioned by the relevant interaction of solar-radiational-fragmentation, coupled with low-altitude ice crystal formations due to atmospheric ionization and temperature inversion productive of the phenomenon commonly categorized as "Mock Sun" or "Sun Dog" well known to scientists and frequently appertaining to mountainous areas.

The subsequent accelerated upward movement of these alleged cloud formations following immediately upon a period of non-activity would be occasioned by intensified thermic-current-fluctuation due to instability inherent in conditional-humidity-responses associated with mountainous-adjacent-to-desert terrain. But although this particular category of cloud-density-luminence-fluctuation has not previously been reported nor observed within the Province, it is not totally unfamiliar within the purview of other Areas outside the Observational-Establishment-Facilities of this Department where the Observer-emotive-impact-factor would be minimalized accordingly.

D.B.M.

For and on Behalf of
Director. Met.

Death Certificate

PRAETORIVM, IERVSALEM

(Forma B/XXV/IV)

NAME   Sylvanvs, Marcvs. M. (former Captain, Special Service)

NATVRE OF DEATH
Military Execution.

DATE   a.d. XIII Kal. Dec. DCCIIC

OFFENCE(S) (Delete if not applicable)
(I)   Treason
(II)   Defection in the line of Duty

CARRIED OVT   *O.H.M.*   WITNESSED   *P.S.L.*

Copies to:— (I)   Registrar of Births, Deaths and Marriages
(Caesarea)

(II)   Records. G.H.Q.
(III)   Office of the Most Holy Inquisition.

OFFICE OF THE MOST HOLY INQUISITION

The Deputy Director acknowledges with thanks the Receipt (for his Records) of the DEATH CERTIFICATE of:—

"Marcvs Sylvanvs", former Captain in the Special Service, executed on Kislev 29:—

"For Treason and Defection in the line of Duty" which we have been empowered to suppress in its totality.

H.H.

p.p. SAUL OF TARSUS L.L.B.
Barrister-at-Law
Deputy Director of The Most Holy Office.

(Signed in Absentio, as he is now on
the road to Damascus.)

NO FURTHER
ACTION

OFFICE FOR COLONIAL AFFAIRS

a.d. X Kal. Sept. A.U.C. MLXXXII

PRIVATE AND CONFIDENTIAL

Paulus Agricola,
Secretary,
H.M. Controller of Records
Records Dept.
Home Office,
Via Imperia. Roma, Insula IV.

My Dear Paulus,

I have studied the "Jesus File" most carefully. I have also been in the Civil Service for a very long time and have long ago reached the unshakable opinion that there is nothing more calculated to disrupt its smooth operation, and nothing *less* likely to win you advancement, than to initiate something that your duties do not require of you.

The file in question would be of little more than historical and academic interest were it not an open secret that Her Majesty, Helena, the Queen Mother is more than interested in this growing Christian Cult; and I am beset by disturbing rumours (but keep this strictly to yourself!) that she is mounting a full scale archaeological expedition to Judaea to dig around for any relics and evidence which might in the aggregate influence His Imperial Majesty to go "considerably further" than his recent repeal of the Penal Laws. This is somewhat depressing, for it could well mean that we might possibly be obliged to adapt ourselves (temporarily I hope) to a brand new State religion lacking the fun, the tolerance and the boisterous adventures of the Gods of Rome, with all their delightfully vague and improbable theology. But tiresome as this could be, I truthfully cannot see it lasting very long.

It's all been tried before!

There was an Egyptian King, "Akenatonvs" who tried to set up a "One-God-Only" type of religion. But it didn't last. The Jews tried it (with slightly more success) and look what happened to them. Where are they now? Scattered, dispersed like chaff while Rome – Eternal Rome – remains. People got bored with it. You must have Gods in all shapes and sizes; Gods to suit every taste; cosy Gods, homely Gods, something the simple-minded can get their prayers into, and which the sophisticate can enjoy without the effort of faith or affront to intelligence. Frankly, after study ing the papers, this Jesus sounds too much like a *real* God for safety.

Imagine what life would be like if he were to be taken seriously. The Empire would collapse overnight – He said: "Forgive your enemies." Is there to be no justice? Are we to let the enemies of Rome run riot? – He said; "Do good to those that harm you." Are we to let the Barbarians do as they choose with us? Are H.M. Prisons to become happy holiday camps with prizes for the worst offenders? He said: "If a man strikes you, turn the other cheek." Tell *that* to the Legionnaires! Tell that to the owners of expensive slaves!

Disband the Legions? Stand down the ballistic missiles? Scrap the Police and the Secret Police? Free all the slaves? Release all the malefactors? Pardon all the political prisoners? Tell every ignorant oaf to love every other ignorant oaf as much as he loves himself! Tell every fool to believe a God dwells within him capable of achieving all things! – Patricians (possibly???) But pray what kind of a God would care to make his "temple" in the stinking carcase of a Pleb? A very sorry sort of "God" in my view; a sub-standard "God", a poor thing not worthy of consideration.

But perhaps I am being unduly pessimistic. For if, as a result of this Council of Trent, Rome should conceivably endorse this peculiar religion it would automatically come under the discipline of our magnificent Legal System, and there, codified, pruned and purged of every irregularity, would find any resemblance to its amazing founder smoothly ironed out.

This Jesus may or may not have contrived to rise from the tomb. But this vociferous and turbulent council, presently taking place (I hear rival bishops have even come to blows) will soon take care of that. Once it is over and receives the Imperial Imprimatur, the unfortunate carpenter's son will be reburied – this time perm-anently under such a mountain of good Roman Law that not even he could succeed in a second resurrection!

No, my dear Paulus, don't fret yourself. Though youthful, our Constantine is wise for his tender years. He will patiently chair this ridiculous Council; force them to come to terms and to agree on some formula which will modify and contain these hopelessly idealistic and impractical doctrines within a "Fail-safe" framework acceptable to State Security.

But whatever happens let us not be party to it. Not that I believe for one moment there is any real danger, the Civil Service will see to that! But Emperors are Emperors and when they have religious maniacs for mothers their whims *can* be dangerous. Therefore, Old Friend, we shall stay on the safe side. I am promptly consigning the "Jesus File" to the vaults, Declassified, and marked for all time: "NO FURTHER ACTION". There let it collect the cobwebs it deserves.

Meanwhile, join us in our box on Thursday at the circus. Wicked old Julia is coming and has some really delicious new scandals to relate.

In True Friendship
PUBLIUS FLAVIUS

DE-CLASSIFIED

CASE FINALISED

NO FURTHER ACTION

RETURN TO VAULT